Jealousy Monsters

Starlight Investigations - Book 1

Marnie Atwell

First Edition printed in America 2016
Second Edition printed in Australia 2020

ISBN: 978-0-6450281-0-2

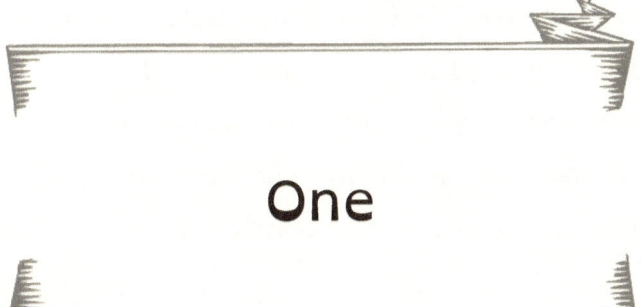

One

Scout closed her eyes and let her psyche communicate with nature. She was looking for anomalies that would indicate where her next job lay, and hoped it would be somewhere out in the country. The beach was a nice place to visit, but it had left her feeling raw and depleted after a week's stay. Scout had specific needs to stay healthy.

MARNIE ATWELL

She required plenty of moonlight to recharge her magic, which she could find anywhere. A close proximity to bushland to pick the fresh mushrooms that littered the forest floor providing physical nourishment, and a clean flowing stream to provide spiritual stimulation. The salty air and the constant bombardment of sand wreaked havoc with her state of mind, and made it difficult for her to do her job effectively. Next time she would request the services of a fellow Locator, but doubted anyone would put their hand up voluntarily, *she wouldn't*.

No way was she going to get a clear reading this close to the coastline. She needed to fly up into the hinterlands, where the atmospheric waves were calmer and less cluttered with the oppressive nature of busy humans. They always seemed to be in a rush. They hardly ever took the time to stop and have a good look at their surroundings. Always too busy chasing their next dollar to buy things they didn't really need. Therein lay the problem.

JEALOUSY MONSTERS

The busyness of the humans created marvellous opportunities for the creatures that preyed on them, to take what they needed, then move on undetected. That was the reason she, and others of her kind, had been placed on this planet. They had an instinct for locating those monsters, and this had now become her full-time job.

Scout didn't miss her homeland when she was able to live in the woods, as the woods on Earth were very similar to her surroundings back home. Her kind lived in mushroom shaped houses that were situated in a circle, much like the mushroom rings found on Earth. She didn't care much for the homes that humans lived in. Their rooms were too rigid in shape, and didn't allow for the natural flow of energy, which the fairies relied on to function effectively.

As a Locator Fairy, she lived a lonely, nomadic life. Sometimes she was able to team up with another Locator Fairy to take care of a situation, but these opportunities were few and far between. She actually preferred to work on her own, because she found it hard to say goodbye to her partner at the end of a case, and felt even lonelier than she did before.

Scout arrived at the outskirts of town, and already felt better. She could see the trees just ahead, and chose one to rest her weary wings. It had been a long flight, but worth the energy to get some peace. Her last job had been difficult. She had nearly lost the child being targeted, and he had suffered great traumatic stress. He was currently in the care of specialist doctors, and she hoped he would make a full recovery. She had done her part in keeping him alive, now the specialists needed to do theirs.

The Collectors had come swiftly once Force, her Gatherer, had contained the creature, and she had been extremely grateful. It sometimes took a few days for them to travel the distance between their planet, Mystique, which was situated in a far off universe, and the Earth. There were a number of hidden portals, special doorways, between the two planets, but Scout was not privy to their locations. Only the

JEALOUSY MONSTERS

Collectors were able to find and operate the portals between worlds.

She had tried to follow them once but they were sneaky. They had come across curious Locators many times over the previous centuries, and were adept at losing a tail. After a few attempts, she had decided to give up on the idea of finding one, and chose to concentrate on her task of protecting the humans. Scout had a knack for finding the monsters that targeted children. She didn't have any children of her own, neither was she in a hurry to create one.

Though if she did, there would be no question as to what the faeling would look like. It would simply be a smaller version of her. Silky smooth skin in a luscious, cream colour. Lilac coloured hair and irises, with strawberry coloured lips. A delicate, pink glow that highlighted beautiful cheekbones. Delicate, blue and purple wings with black spots patterned like a peacock's tail attached near her shoulder blades.

MARNIE ATWELL

The young start out as the size of a grain of rice and over the next twelve months, grow to be no taller than the length of an adult human's middle finger. Scout's wardrobe consisted of strapless tops that were the same colour as her hair, with full length black trousers, and flat, strapped sandals. As these colours were her staple, she would, of course, place any children she chose to have, in clothing that also had lilac and black colouring.

Scout considered the children that she watched and shadowed to be her own, for the short time it took to locate the monsters and have them carted away. For now, that was enough for her. Some of the children were quite cute and she often enjoyed listening to them talking to their toys, dolls and action figures, as though they were real. She was amazed at the resilience of the younger humans and the insights they revealed.

The other type of children was what stopped her from wanting to have some of her own. They were so nasty and self-absorbed, that she couldn't wait for the Collectors to come, as she was fearful she would give those horrible, selfish children to the monsters herself.

That was one of the difficulties of her job. Scout was not supposed to have an opinion about anything, and she struggled with that objective all the time. The monsters were real, and they took great pleasure in torturing children, sometimes even killing them. But Force and she weren't allowed to hurt the creatures. Supposedly, everything had a right to life, which was why the creatures were relocated instead of being terminated. The creatures were just trying to survive, too.

She would be in so much trouble if her supervisors knew she called them monsters. It was a bit hard not to, when the children she tried to protect called them that, all the time. She would hear them telling their parents there was a monster under their bed or a monster in their closet.

MARNIE ATWELL

It didn't matter how many times it happened, Scout would become angry with the parents for not believing their children.

She watched them check under the bed, or open the wardrobe telling the children there was nothing there. Then they would tell the children to go to sleep, and walk out of the room, turning the light off as they went. Her blood would boil, and she wanted to storm in there and tell the parents how it really was, but she never did.

Thanks to the Locators, Gatherers and Collectors, adults had forgotten living in a world where they were so terrified by the unimaginable creatures that walked the Earth, that some people actually died of fright. She often reminded herself that the adults didn't know about the creatures, because the Battle Stars had cleansed the planet three thousand years ago, and imprisoned the creatures on their planet, Mystique.

Their Queen had gathered a group of her best Battle Stars, and asked them to return to Earth to guard the humans against any creatures that had been left behind, or ventured to come. She told them they would henceforth be known as the Gatherers. They would be assisted by a group of fairies able to sense the vile creatures. These would become known as the Locators. She gave her new Gatherers the ability to contact another elite group of warriors, who would remain on Mystique with her. These Battle Stars, referred to as the Collectors, would return to Earth, once contacted, to relocate the captured creatures.

The sole purpose of the Locators being on Earth, was to give the humans a chance of living their life without true fear. It was their mission to find the creatures that were tormenting the humans, and contact their Gatherer when the creature had been located.

The Gatherers' task was to capture the creatures and contain them for collection by the Collectors. The Collectors were tasked with relocating the creatures, captured by the Gatherers, to the planet, Mystique. There they would be handed over to the Battle Star teams, who spent their working day ensuring the creatures were unable to escape their allocated zones, and find their way back to Earth.

Scout made herself comfortable on the branch of the tree, and let her psyche drift to connect with nature. Everything was calm within the nearest two kilometres. She cast her power out a bit further, then a bit further again, until she was fifty kilometres away. There was a ripple to the north-west, so she gathered in her net, and concentrated her search in that area. The ripple became a small wave, as she extended another twenty-five kilometres.

Scout opened her eyes and got to her feet. She had found her next contract, and called her favourite Gatherer. "Hi, Force. I've located a monster seventy-seven kilometres north-west of my current location. Are you available?"

"Yes, I just finished a case. I'll check the local newspapers to see if there is anything to pinpoint what you are sensing," replied Force.

JEALOUSY MONSTERS

"Thanks, Force. Let me know what you find." She flew down to the forest floor to get something to eat. In the middle of a small clearing was a joey, a baby kangaroo, which had recently left its mother's pouch.

The joey eyed her warily as she approached. Scout moved slowly, not wanting to scare it away. It was standing within a couple of metres of a scrumptious looking mushroom ring. The tops of the mushrooms were light brown in colour, and the flesh underneath was a gorgeous dusty-pink. They were her favourite, and she wanted to fill her little satchel with them before she left at nightfall.

The joey decided she was not a threat, and went back to grazing, no longer paying her any attention. She broke off a small piece of mushroom and delicately placed it in her mouth.

It was so delicious, she soon discovered she had stuffed her face until her stomach was bloated and it hurt to move. There was a waterfall nearby. Scout could hear the water roaring over the rocks, and walked painfully towards the sound. She wasn't going to make it. 'Not to worry,' she told herself and flew up to the closest branch where she wrapped herself in a leaf, and slept for a couple of hours.

The sound of the waterfall rejuvenated her spirit as she slept. Her dreams were full of flowers, rainbows, and little girls with big eyes and pig tails, and little boys with cheeky smiles and dirty hands. The earpiece, that she had forgotten to take out before she went to sleep, started buzzing. It was Force calling with some information.

"Scout, there have been six children aged between twelve and fourteen who have disappeared in the past six months. Their bodies have not been found, and there has been no evidence left behind at any of the scenes."

"Are they all from the same area?" she asked.

"They are from different suburbs, but belong to the same district," he answered. "And get this, they have all disappeared between the twelfth and fourteenth of the month."

"Hmmm, that *is* interesting. What do the adults think?"

"They think the children have been taken by members of a religious cult."

"Why do they think that?" she asked.

"The families reported the children had seemed to change before they disappeared, but when they had asked the kids what was wrong, they were told everything was fine."

"What do you mean by 'changed'?" she asked.

"I don't know. I've made an appointment with two of the children's parents for this afternoon. I'll talk to the locals and let you know what they have to say. Are you leaving at dusk?" he asked, knowing she preferred to travel when there were fewer predators in the sky.

"Just after. I should reach the area around ten."

"Be careful. There are a lot of foxes, wild dogs and owls out in that part of the country," he stated.

"Thanks. Hey, Force, when is the twelfth?"

"Tomorrow."

"Oh! That's not good. What day is it tomorrow?"

"Saturday."

"So, the kids won't be at school then?"

"Nope. Scout, I've got to get to these meetings. I'll meet up with you tomorrow morning, okay?"

"Okay," she said as he hung up.

Now that she was rested and the bulge in her tummy had gone down a bit, she flew to the waterfall and dipped her fingers in. The water was cool and fresh, so she flew to the edge of the calm section, then undressed and stepped in. The water was glorious on her skin.

She saw a nutshell lying nearby, and thanked the human who had left it behind, so she could use it to wash her clothes. She rubbed the shell up and down the material of her outfit while it lay beneath the water. She wrung her lilac coloured, strapless shirt and black dress pants out, and left them on a warm rock to dry while she bathed herself.

JEALOUSY MONSTERS

A fairy's skin was self-cleaning, as long as there was enough clean water to make it damp, but she swam just for the sheer pleasure of feeling her arms and legs move in harmony. Scout climbed out of the water and gave herself a shake. Once the water droplets had been dispersed, the pores in her skin released fairy dust, which rose in a cloud of yellow sparkles. Her skin glowed with health, her purple hair darkened to almost black, and her lilac eyes shone with happiness. Playtime was over, she had a job to get to.

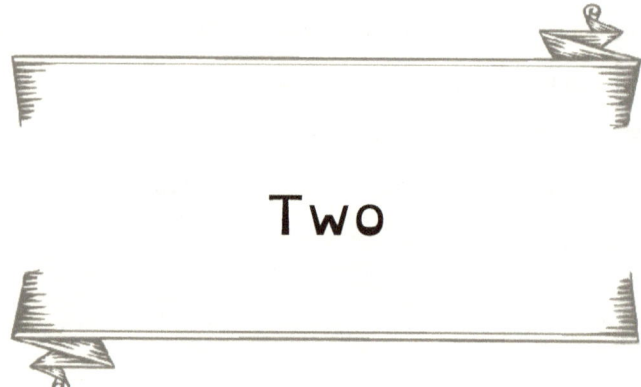

Two

Force visited two of the families who had gone through the trauma of having their children go missing. The first was the mother of a thirteen-year-old boy, named Michael, who had been taken on the thirteenth of last month. The second was the father of a fourteen-year-old girl, named Belinda, who was taken on the fourteenth of the month before.

JEALOUSY MONSTERS

Michael's mum, Katrina, heard him arrive on his motorcycle and looked out the window to see who had pulled up in her front yard. She admired the young man who sported a buzz cut, but shook her head in disapproval at him for not wearing a helmet. She stared as he swung his leg over the seat and smiled with pleasure as his long, black pants stretched tightly across his bottom. He removed his leather jacket and placed it over the handlebars.

Katrina nodded with approval at the black singlet that hugged the man's chest and revealed his sculpted arms. She wondered, fleetingly, if the man might be one of those dangerous bikies that the media kept warning the public about, then quickly dismissed the idea. Someone that good looking couldn't possibly be up to no good.

Katrina hurried to the door and, throwing caution to the wind, flung open the door as he reached the top of the stairs. She was a little taken aback when she looked into his eyes and found them to be a strange coral colour, which did not look normal, at all. She became frightened of him and went to close the door when he picked up on her thoughts.

"Wait," he implored, raising his hand to each eye as if removing contact lenses. He changed his eyes to a dark shade of brown, and pretended to pocket the lenses in his pants pocket. "They are not real. When I wear them, the kids say I look like one of the Cullens in Twilight. It helps me break the ice with them, so I can gather information."

He held out his hand for a handshake and said, "Hi, my name is Liam Force and I am a private investigator with Starlight Investigations. I am looking into the disappearance of your son, Michael, and have been given the task of developing a profile on the victims, so the police can get a better understanding of what they might be dealing with."

Katrina asked him to come in as she wrung her hands nervously. He noticed the stress lines around her nose and mouth. The pain in the depths of her grey coloured eyes that showed the woman was beginning to run out of hope of ever seeing her son alive again. Michael had only been missing a month, and yet, the yellow t-shirt and black pair of shorts she had on, were already looking two sizes too big. Her caramel coloured hair, lacking in lustre, was scraped back in a messy pony tail.

"The police report mentioned you had noticed some changes in Michael just before he went missing, and that he seemed a little off. Would you be able to clarify that statement at all?" Force asked her.

"Michael had seemed a little angry in the couple of weeks preceding his disappearance," Katrina replied. "I wasn't able to get to the root of the problem. He suddenly stopped confiding in me about everything that was going on in his life."

"Did you notice or implement any changes to Michael's routine?"

"No. Everything seemed normal, up until the moment I noticed he was missing. He went to school, came home, did his homework and followed that up with his chores. Then we had dinner, but he wouldn't tell me anything anymore. Michael would just grunt at me if I asked him a question, and he stopped volunteering information. After he ate, he would place his dishes in the sink then have his bath.

"Most nights he went to his room and read a book. A couple of times, he sat out here and watched some television for an hour before going to bed. On the weekends he was allowed to play with his friends until lunch time, after he had completed his morning chores. After lunch, he helped out at the local library for a couple of hours, and then the afternoon was his until it was time to feed and milk the cows before dinner."

"Would you mind if I take a look in Michael's room?" he asked her.

Katrina's heart lurched in her chest at the thought of another human being entering Michael's private space. Her hesitation in allowing him access, led him to pull out all of the tricks of persuasion he knew. The fact that he was the only person who had asked to see Michael's things, which might lead to finding a clue, finally gained him entrance.

"Thank you, Katrina. Would you like to come in while I investigate?"

"No, thank you. Could you please try not to make too much of a mess? I have kept everything the way it was before Michael disappeared, so it will be the same for him if he returns."

The room was spacious. They lived in a one story home, and Michael's bedroom was on the north-east corner. There were windows on two of the walls, a wardrobe on the other, and his bed sat against the fourth. His bedroom had an Avengers theme, with bedspread, pillow case and matching curtains.

There were a couple of shelves on the wall beside the windows on the southern side, which held an assortment of Avengers figurines and a photo in a frame of Michael and his parents. Michael looked very much like his father, having lightly waving brown hair, hazel eyes and both

21

wearing glasses. His built-in wardrobe had a mirror as one of the sliding doors, and a poster of Captain America on the other.

The room was tidy and organised, with nothing out of place. He was either a very neat teenager, or his mother cleaned his room for him every day. There was a hook on the wall, with nothing on it. He left the room to find Katrina crying at the kitchen table. As he walked into the room, she got up to put the kettle on, asking if he would like a tea or coffee. Force asked for a coffee, not feeling thirsty, but realizing Katrina needed something to do to help get herself under control.

"What is the hook in Michael's room for?" Force asked.

"That's where he hangs his bag when he gets home from school," Katrina answered.

"When was the last time Michael was seen?"

"In the afternoon of the thirteenth of September, when he got off the school bus after school."

"Have you spoken to the bus driver?"

22

"Yes, but he said he hadn't seen anyone in the vicinity when he dropped Michael off. Also, he was the only child to get off at that bus stop on the day."

"Katrina, do you know the names of Michael's friends who might catch the bus home with him?"

"Why are you asking all of these questions? I have already told the police everything I know and it should be in that police report you have."

"I am trying to see if the police missed something at the time, or if you have remembered something since your interview with them. I am sorry if I am upsetting you," he said gently.

"I'm sorry I was so short with you. I know you are trying to help." She took a deep breath and continued, "This is a small country town, and everybody knows everybody and everybody else's business. The kids he hangs out with the most are Ronald, Gary and Theo. Gary and Theo catch the bus with him, Ronald gets a lift with his dad."

"Did Michael have a falling out with any of his friends?"

"I don't know. He stopped confiding in me, remember!" she snapped. Closing her eyes for a moment, she took a breath to calm herself, then let it out. "Sorry. He mentioned a girl named Ruby and a boy named Lucas who were new to town, just before he decided to clam up on me. He said they were home-schooled by their parents. He kept bugging me about being allowed to cut down on his chores so he could visit these kids after school.

"I felt really bad at having to tell him no. It's just him and me now. I can't afford to pay someone to help me keep the farm running. Actually, it was around that time that he began giving me a hard time, and cutting me out of his life," she told Force.

"Did Michael happen to mention where Ruby and Lucas live?"

"No."

JEALOUSY MONSTERS

"Thank you for going over this again with me, Katrina. Can you tell me where I can find Ronald, Gary, and Theo?"

She gave him directions to the Mitchells and the Andersons who might be able to shed some more light onto the situation. He wrote his mobile number on his business card and handed it to Katrina.

"Call me if you think of anything else that might help. Thanks for your time. I'll contact you as soon as I find out what has happened to Michael." Katrina held back a sob as she took the card from him, appreciating the fact he hadn't told her he would bring Michael home soon. Neither of them knew if he could do that or not, and she was glad he hadn't made a promise he may not be able to keep. She hoped he had more luck in jogging the memories of Ronald, Gary and Theo than she had.

Force rode the short distance to Ronald's house to be told the kids were at the Anderson's. He nodded his thanks, and found his way without much effort. The people around there were excellent at giving directions, and he soon found himself watching the boys mucking out the stables.

Two of the boys were clearly brothers with light brown hair, brown eyes and a dimple that perched on their left cheeks. They wore light blue jeans and a flannel shirt, one in blue/black, the other in green/black. Black sneakers finished off their outfits. The other boy had blonde hair whose fringe hung over his eyes, making it hard to determine the colour of his eyes. He wore a pair of black jodhpurs, a cream coloured, long sleeved shirt, and black riding boots.

"G'day boys, how's it going?" Force called to them.

"We aren't allowed to talk to strangers," replied Ronald.

Force held out his fake badge for them to see, and told them their parents had told him where to find them. The kids came over to take a look, and asked him what he wanted.

"I'm looking into the disappearance of Michael Golding. You boys know him?"

"Yeah, I've known him since before we could talk," replied Ronald. "Our parents have been friends since their school days."

"So you were close with him then?" asked Force.

"Nah, they were sworn enemies. Well, as far as Michael was concerned anyway," replied Gary.

"Yeah? Why was that?" Force enquired.

"He seemed to have some jealousy issues with Ronald and his parents. He was always going on about it when Ronald wasn't around," Gary said.

"It was really sad," Theo said. "He kept going on about how Ronald didn't appreciate his parents like he should. I've never met a kid who appreciated his parents more. Michael's Mum loved him a lot, you know. It was too bad his dad died in February. Cancer, you know. Now she's lost them both."

"Did you boys ever meet a couple of kids named Ruby and Lucas? Apparently, they are not from around here."

"No, haven't heard of them," Ronald replied.

"Heard Michael mention them once," Theo said. "They are a few years older than us, and he liked that they took an interest in him. I'm pretty sure he said they were too old for school."

"How come you haven't met them?" Force asked.

"Michael wanted to keep them all to himself," Theo answered. "Made him feel better than us, I think."

"What do you think happened to Michael?" Force asked them.

"Don't know," replied the three of them.

He gave them each a copy of his card, and asked them to ring him if they thought of anything else. He turned to leave then remembered the bus driver. "What about the bus driver?"

"Carl?" questioned Theo.

"He's cool. Real protective, you know," said Gary.

JEALOUSY MONSTERS

"Carl wouldn't hurt any of us, and certainly wouldn't drop us off and leave us, if he thought we might be in danger," Theo said.

Force felt the truth of their conviction, and nodded his head. "Take care of each other, and don't wander the streets on your own."

The boys watched him leave wide-eyed. "Did you see the muscles on that guy?" Theo queried.

"Yep, he's ripped," replied the other two.

Ronald looked at the card: *Starlight Investigations, Liam Force, Phone: 1800 Starlight.*

Force returned to his motorbike and rode to the home that Belinda had lived in. He was met at the door by Belinda's dad, Darren, and his blue cattle dog who was barking ferociously.

"Be quiet, Woofer," Darren said to the dog. "What can I do for ya?" he asked the stranger.

"I'd like to talk to you about Belinda, if I could," Force said holding up his badge.

"I already told the police everythin' I know," Darren said and turned away.

"I've got a new lead I would like to discuss with you," Force said raising his voice to be heard.

Darren turned back and stared at Force for a few seconds. He walked back to the screen door and said, "Whatcha found?"

Force looked at him for a couple of minutes to make a decision on how to proceed, now that he had the man's attention. He looked to be about forty-five years old but was probably ten years younger than that. Working the land and spending so much time in the sun, could sometimes make a person look a lot older than they were.

His hair was thinning on top, and there were some grey strands peppered through the red hairs of his beard. The depth of his emotional pain could be felt when looking into his green coloured eyes, and the lines around his mouth, confirmed his heartbreak.

He wore a pair of dark blue jeans with black, steel capped boots. His dark blue flannel shirt was rolled up at the sleeves and was unbuttoned to reveal a white t-shirt underneath. Force could feel the seeds of hope beginning to germinate and hoped he would be able to bring Darren a happy ending. "May I come in?"

"No, I'll come out. Woofer don't like strangers in the house," he said stepping outside. Darren indicated a chair for Force to sit in, then moved his chair to keep his face out of the sun, and joined him. "So, whatcha got?"

"Do you remember Belinda talking about a girl called Ruby and a boy named Lucas?"

"No, can't say as I do. Are they kids at school?"

"Apparently, they are home-schooled by their parents. They encouraged the other missing children to catch up with them after school, before they disappeared," Force replied.

"Do you think my Belinda has run away with these kids?"

"I don't know. Do you?"

"It's possible," Darren mused. "I got together with the other parents when my Belinda went missin'. They felt it mighta been a religious cult thing. You know, adults brainwashin' our kids into thinkin' we was bad or somethin'. Now, thinkin' that kids mighta stole my Belinda away, kinda makes sense. She would be more willin' to go with a coupl'a kids."

"Do you know who Belinda's closest friends are? I would like to have a chat with them to see if they know anything about these two kids."

"Yeah, sure. Tamara Jones. She lives two k's up the road. Take a right and follow that for another kilometre, turn left, and the driveway is three hundred metres on ya right."

"Thanks, Darren. I'll let you know as soon as I find her, and the people that took her. Here's my card. Call me if you think of anything else."

Force's mind searched for Tamara's current location, while his eyes returned to their normal colour. He discovered she was playing with a couple of girls in the park. When he arrived, he showed them his badge and they answered his questions, after remarking how cool his eyes were and indicating they would like to go for a ride on his motorcycle. Belinda had not been a very nice girl, or so it seemed. She picked on Tamara all the time. Tamara didn't know why, but when asked if she was glad that Belinda wasn't there anymore, he was surprised by her answer.

"Belinda is an angry girl who wants people to like her, but doesn't know how to make them. She doesn't understand that you can't *make* friends like you. They just do, or don't," Tamara said.

"Belinda was jealous of Tamara's relationship with her parents," her friend, Sarah, told Force.

"I wish Belinda hadn't gone missing," Tamara told him. "I hoped that we could have become friends, and would like to have invited her for a sleepover."

"Have you girls seen any new kids in the area?"

"No."

"Have you heard Belinda mention a Ruby or Lucas?"

"No, sorry we haven't," Sarah answered, checking with the other girls first.

Force said goodbye to the girls, and returned to the room he had rented above the Pub. He turned on the computer and jumped on the internet to do some research. There seemed to be a common thread which involved feelings of jealousy. He hoped to be able to find something that would give him a better understanding of what he and Scout were up against, and how to deal with it. He was meeting her in the morning, and she would expect him to have formulated a plan of action, to take care of the threat.

Three

Scout found that there were fewer dangers travelling at night than there were during the day. Nocturnal creatures hunted her, too, but they were fewer in number than the diurnal predators, although they were harder to see coming.

Usually, she heard them just before their talons could hook into her soft, delicate skin. So far, she had been able to manoeuvre herself to avoid capture. She didn't want to become anything's dinner.

Scout avoided high-traffic streets as much as possible. The streetlights and headlights caught the fairy dust in its beams and made it glow radiantly, bringing unwanted attention. Scout tried to keep to the backroads as much as possible. She preferred to stay away from houses as well.

Pets usually sensed her nearby, and created a ruckus. Dogs were the most annoying with their incessant barking, but cats were the more dangerous predator. Some felines sat in the windows, watching and waiting for their chance to pounce. She wasn't particularly worried about housecats, with the safety of glass between them and her. If the cat was outside, however, well now, that was a different kettle of fish.

They were incredible hunters, and she had found herself in the grip of a black cat's mouth once. What a scary night that had been. She had only managed to get away by shaking herself hard to coat the cat's tongue in fairy dust. He'd spat her out in disgust and ran off, hacking and wheezing. Apart from a mild headache from shaking herself so much, she'd escaped without injury.

Scout flew toward her destination very carefully. She conserved her energy, by flying for an hour then resting for fifteen minutes, and arrived just shy of ten o'clock. She spent the night committing the layout of the town to memory. She flew into each open window to see who lived in each house.

Most of the parents were already in bed fast asleep, but some were still wide awake. She had to be very careful in those homes, especially if they had pets. There were many homes that contained children, but only seven that she had been able to enter, had children in the right age bracket. Four girls and three boys had just made their way on to her list of possible targets.

While scouting the area, she had found a beautiful old oak tree. It was like the one she had lived beneath, back home in Fairyland. A few of her favourite mushrooms that she could snack on, grew on the ground beneath the canopy. She found a small hole which led to a hollow in the trunk that she could climb in, and make into her home for a few days.

This was lucky, as there was a storm coming. The clouds quickly strengthened in the west. Although it was too dark to see their colour deepening, she felt the drop in air pressure, and saw the lightning streak its way across the sky towards the town.

Scout flew swiftly from the house she had just vacated, to the park where her makeshift home was located, a couple of blocks away. She grabbed a few leaves from the branches and made a little nest in the hollow, to protect her delicate skin from the harshness of the bark. The sound of the thunder was terrifying. The tree rumbled beneath her body, and she wished she was not alone.

They never had scary storms back in Fairyland, and she still hadn't gotten used to the experience of them on Earth. It used to rain often in Fairyland, and Scout and her sisters would happily practise flying between the raindrops.

They would play hide and seek until their wings became too water-logged to fly anymore. At that time, they would find shallow puddles, and see which ones they could cross from one side to the other, without their heads going under. Scout was a couple of millimetres taller than her family members, and had a great advantage in this game.

It was times like this that she really missed her sisters. How lovely it would have been to huddle together, and tell scary stories about the monsters they had come across, since living on Earth. The storm was a perfect backdrop for such things.

Scout found herself thinking about the monster she had picked up on her radar. She wondered if it knew, somehow, that it was being hunted, and had some sort of power over the weather. Maybe it was using the storm to prevent her from finding its home.

Scout wished she could ring Force and ask him such questions. She knew that if she were to be able to connect to his phone, she wouldn't be able to hear him anyway, with the sound of thunder crackling in the night sky every thirty seconds or so. Worse thoughts just popped into her head.

'What if the lightning hit her tree? Would it catch on fire? Would she explode on impact? Oh my goodness. Should she stay here and run the risk of a lightning strike? Or should she make a dash for it?' Panicked, her breathing quickened and her heart felt like it was going to jump out of her chest.

She tried really hard to slow her breathing. It didn't work. Scout began counting slowly from one to ten, then from ten to fifty, and noticed that concentrating on something else was working. She kept going until she had reached two thousand, and realised the storm's intensity had weakened, and the lightning and thunder were occurring less often. It was also moving further away.

JEALOUSY MONSTERS

She grabbed her satchel and wrapped her arms around it for comfort. She listened to the howl of the wind and the pounding of the rain, with a flash of light and rumble of thunder thrown in for good measure. She had been really tired from flying, and didn't notice her eyes becoming heavy as the rain settled into a steady rhythm. Before she knew it, she had fallen asleep to nature's lullaby.

Scout heard birds chirping and whipped her head around to locate them. Her sudden movement brought her to the attention of the birds who decided she would make a lovely appetiser. The race was on to see which bird would get to her first. Scout flew for her life. Her legs moved as though they were running in an attempt to give her wings more speed. She felt the snap of a beak right behind her head and her eyes flew open in fright. Panting in fear, she realised she had been dreaming.

Scout had climbed her way to the top of the hole in the trunk of her tree. As her fear subsided, her legs relaxed and she found herself sliding down the curve on a bed of leaves. She screamed with fear and held a leaf tightly in front of her body as she whooshed out of her home and landed in the middle of a spider's web, glistening with raindrops from the storm. The web tore in the corner as it flexed to hold her weight. Scout found herself tumbling in the web which had effectively rolled the leaves so that they wrapped around her body, trapping her inside.

Her weight had not been enough to destroy the web completely, so she had found herself suspended in the air, unable to break free. Her squeals of fear had drawn the attention of a mother bird who had been feeding her babies. She had flown down to investigate the source of the noise inside the leaves by poking them with her beak.

Scout kept still and hoped the bird would go away. It did, but then flew back in for another look. It kept coming and going as it was unable to hover in the one spot, until making the decision to slice through the thread that kept her dangling from the tree. Down, down, down she fell, then up, up, up she went as the bird flew away with her. The mother bird placed her in the base of its nest as the babies squawked with joy. She carefully opened the leaves, and stared as Scout was revealed.

"What is that?" asked the oldest baby bird.

"I'm not eating that," said the other.

"I don't know what it is," said the mother bird, "but it seems to be missing a couple of legs. Just try it, you might like it."

"No, I don't want to. Can't we have some worms?" they chorused in unison.

"You will eat what you are given," the mother bird stated.

"Nope, that looks disgusting," replied the youngest bird receiving a wing to its chest from the first hatchling.

"Please, mother, can we have some worms?" the oldest fledgling asked sweetly.

"Fine," said the mother bird as she flew off in a huff to find a lovely garden to scratch around in.

The little birds stared at Scout, while Scout stared at the little birds, which weren't so little compared to her, and considered how lucky she had just been. She gave the baby magpies a wave and flew away, too.

The morning had barely started, and the children should still be asleep. Scout found her bearings and flew back to her tree. She grabbed the satchel and ate some of the pieces of mushroom for breakfast, while pondering her best plan of attack.

The area was too large to follow the trail of missing children. Force would be doing that anyway, and she would just be doubling up and wasting energy. She decided her best bet was to look for the creature's aura trail, and to try to discover where it spent most of its time.

The monster seemed to prefer pre and young teenagers, so she needed to discover where they liked to hang out in this area. Parks, sporting grounds, the river, dams and stables were probably their most likely haunts, she decided. She couldn't think of any others, but thought that was plenty of places to get started on her search. As her tree was in a park, she decided to start there.

She picked up on a fine mist of green that swirled gently around the monkey bars, and headed off towards the river. The swirl was a bit thicker and deeper in colour at the river. She followed its trail, and found it flicked off towards a dirt road. Wondering where it was leading her, she followed it down a dip and then back up a hill. Round a tree and under a decaying log it went.

She could smell it now. It was bitter and acidic, and she knew the trail was recent. Scout flew faster. The creature had probably selected its target, and she needed to find it before it could snatch the child. Up over another hill, and she realised she was headed towards the child's home near the tree she had stayed in last night. Groaning to herself, she continued with the trail and found herself outside the home she had left, just before the storm hit. The mist was thick and smelt horrible.

Scout felt her heart drop in her chest, and felt like throwing up.

This place belonged to a young girl with blonde hair which had been tied into a bun on each side of her head by her mother, before she went to bed. While Scout had been there, the tween must have dreamed something funny, because she had heard muffled giggles coming from the child, which had brought a smile to her own lips. She could see why the creature might want to take this girl.

She was adorable, even with her eyes closed. Anyone who made noises like that, had to be a beautiful person on the inside. Scout was determined the creature wasn't going to get this one. Now she just had to work out where the creature lived, and what type of monster it was. She would have to keep an eye on this little beauty while she waited to hear from Force.

Four

Scout waited patiently on a branch of a tree in the backyard, watching for signs of movement from within the house. She sat still for half an hour before she heard the girl wake, and detected the sound of her feet hitting the floor.

After a few minutes, the curtains in the bedroom slid back on their runners to reveal the girl's young face at the window. Her hair was messy and her cheeks were flushed from being under the warm covers. Her eyes were a brilliant blue, indicating she was wide awake. This young lady was the prettiest pre-teen Scout had ever seen, and she felt her protective instincts go into overdrive.

The girl had changed out of her 'Frozen' pyjamas, and put on a long sleeved, pink and white shirt, short, pale pink skirt, with dark pink tights beneath. She couldn't see the girl's shoes, but assumed they would be some sort of jogger or high-top, also in pink. The girl opened the window to let the fresh air into her room, then bounded down the stairs for breakfast.

Scout jumped off the branch, and her wings flapped furiously, allowing her feet to gently touch the ground. They carried her to the hedge beneath the kitchen window, where she could remain unseen. Her parents had heard the girl stomping past their room, and woke with the realisation they had slept in. Her mum and dad quickly threw on their business suits, ran a comb through their hair, then met her in the kitchen downstairs. Scout listened to the girl talking to her parents as her dad went about getting her breakfast.

"Sorry, Jacinta, but we have to be on the road in half an hour at the latest. This morning, we are presenting our new housing development project to future clients, at a seminar organised by our company," he said. "What are you planning on doing today?"

"I've arranged to meet my friends down the street at the park a couple of blocks away at seven-thirty," Jacinta replied. "We'll probably hang there for a little while, shooting hoops and playing with the soccer ball. Then we might head down to the canal to see what the fishermen are catching. If the fish are biting, we might come back and pick up our gear, and do a little fishing ourselves."

"Fish are usually on the bite at dawn and dusk," her dad reminded her.

She smiled at him and said, "The girls probably won't want to fish anyway. They might get smelly," she whispered behind her hand.

He howled with laughter and told her to be careful. Standing, he ruffled her hair while she ate her cornflakes, then headed to the bathroom to clean his teeth.

Her mother kissed her on the top of her head, and apologised for not having the time to braid her hair. Remembering Jacinta felt that being twelve was now too old to have pig tails, she replaced the messy buns with neater ones. "Love you, Jacinta. You be careful, now."

"See you, Squirt," Dad said, popping his head back inside to see what was taking his wife so long.

Once her parents had left, Jacinta let out a huge sigh. She wished that her morning would go exactly as she had told her parents. Instead, she needed to hurry up and leave, before the girls were sitting outside, waiting to torment her. She didn't know why they disliked her so much. It had been that way for as long as she had lived there. A long and soul destroying six months.

A couple of weeks ago, their ringleader had taken to phoning her at home to let fly with a string of abuse, until she'd stopped taking her calls. Jacinta learned to be inventive when giving her parents excuses, as to why she couldn't talk to her at that precise minute. She always finished by saying, 'Tell her I will see her at school tomorrow,' which always seemed to satisfy her parents' curiosity, and stopped them from asking probing questions like: Is something going on at school? Or is there a problem between you and Calamity?

Jacinta scoffed the rest of her cereal, and lifted the bowl to her lips so she could chug down the milk. As time was getting away, she didn't bother brushing her teeth and grabbed an apple instead. She squirted peppermint mouth spray to freshen her breath and made certain her house keys were in her backpack, before pulling the door closed behind her.

Her water bottle in hand, she walked over to the hose and, turning on the tap, filled the bottle. She preferred the taste of the water from the hose to the plumbing inside. Some hands of bananas had ripened on the tree, so she pulled off a couple of the ripest ones and placed them in the bag with her water. She grabbed her hat and helmet from the handlebars, and jumped on her bike. As fast as she could, she pedalled down the street hoping that Calamity was still in bed. Unfortunately, her hopes were denied.

Calamity spotted her enemy through the lounge room window as Jacinta rode past. She jumped out of her seat and, with toast in hand, pulled a brush through her hair, picked up her mobile phone and ran out the front door. Phones began ringing all over town. "She's on the move," Calamity told her friends.

"We are rostered on this morning at the stables and have pony club after lunch," Donovan said. William and Justine made noises of agreement.

"I have to be at the church bake sale at eight," Hannah told her. "I can come until seven-thirty."

"Us, too," said Breanna and Jeremy. Their parents were all friends and did a lot of Christian charity work around town. This week's agenda was fundraising for the homeless.

"Don't worry about it," Calamity said in a huff. "Go do your own things. Leave her to me!"

Scout followed as closely to Jacinta as she dared. She knew the girl's name now. That gave her a stronger connection to her, which made it all the more important to keep her safe. Kids like Jacinta, who spent a lot of time on their own, were easy targets for most of the creatures Scout searched for. There were often long periods of time before the children were discovered missing, and there were rarely any witnesses.

Jacinta's parents worked long hours, and quite often left her to fend for herself. Living in a small country town, they believed it was safe for her to travel the streets on her own. Scout hoped she would be able to locate the creature, and that Force would arrive in time to capture it before it took its next victim. She suspected it might be Jacinta.

The stream of the creature's aura had led her to this house, and was quite strong, indicating it had been there for a while. She was disconcerted to find two trails leading to the house from different directions, one male and one female. 'This could be a bad omen,' she thought. They were most likely a breeding pair, and would be stronger together as a result. Luckily, for whatever reason, they had not taken Jacinta yet, but she knew they would return soon, as today was the twelfth of the month.

Since the cleansing of the planet three millennia ago, creatures that had not been caught and sent to Mystique, had separated from their families. Attempting to avoid detection, they ventured out on their own. Every now and then, depending on the species of creature, they would find one another and create new life, to carry on the species' line.

JEALOUSY MONSTERS

After a few centuries, some of the creatures regrouped, thinking they had been forgotten, making it easier for Scout and the other Locators to find them.

This pair was not careful enough to avoid detection by the humans. For some reason, they were hunting in the same area. Something was holding them here, which left a pattern to follow, and encouraged the humans to come together to compare notes.

The Locators were not allowed to harm the creatures, even to protect human lives. They were not to bring attention to themselves, and must remain hidden from humans wherever possible. The Locators were required to make contact with the Gatherers as soon as they registered the existence of a dangerous creature. The situation was to be monitored, and the target removed out of harm's way, whenever deemed necessary.

Dealing with the creatures swiftly and proficiently, was vitally important. It helped to ensure that as many humans as possible, stayed in the dark as to the existence of such creatures on their planet.

If a human was to survive being captured, the Gatherer was required to help them through the trauma they had suffered, and to ensure they understood they were safe. They encouraged the human to keep the knowledge of the creature's existence to themselves. No-one would believe their story and they would surely suffer disbelief and ridicule if they couldn't keep this knowledge to themselves.

Scout remembered asking Force, many years ago, why they didn't just wipe the memory of the incident completely from the human's mind. She thought it was cruel to leave them tortured by the memories of what the creatures had done. It was totally unforgiveable to be unable to discuss what had happened to them with anyone and not having any hope that they'd be believed. Force told her the Royals had made a decree: humans were to remember how terrifying their life had been prior to the cleansing of the Earth.

JEALOUSY MONSTERS

The Monarchy wanted the humans to be humbled, and filled with gratitude, at being saved from the predators that hunted them constantly. They were elated to see their Battle Stars revered as Gods for many centuries after The Cleansing. But, over time, the stories being passed down from one generation of humans to the next, became less impressive, until finally, they were forgotten completely.

The Queen became angry with the humans. She felt helpless as she watched the humans decimate the flora and fauna that were native to their planet. The Queen had not been given the authority to protect the other species of the planet, so she took it upon herself to punish the humans for their arrogance and insolent behaviour.

What Force didn't know, however, was that every couple of months, their Queen would secretly orchestrate a group of creatures to return to Earth to hunt the humans. It appeased her resentment towards the path the humans had taken, and kept her Gatherers and Locators on Earth practised in their craft.

Scout brought her thoughts back to the present. She wondered what was keeping Force. He'd been due to arrive a few minutes ago. She was keen to come up with a strategy for dealing with the creature. Running out of patience, Scout unlocked her phone and gave him a call. "Hey, where are you?" she asked.

"I'm orienting myself with the layout of the town, and am currently at an old barn up in the hills," Force whispered back. "I think I may have stumbled across the creature's stomping grounds. Just give me a minute to see for sure, and I'll let you know my coordinates."

"Force, be careful. There are two of them. I think they might be a mating pair."

He mumbled some choice words, which Scout chose to ignore. She hated it when he swore, but realised she couldn't control what he said. She could only control her own words and actions. When she was silent, he realised he had said the words out loud and apologised.

JEALOUSY MONSTERS

Scout smiled and told him, "Jacinta left a few minutes ago and is being followed by her friend. The creatures' trails led straight to Jacinta's place and I'm sure she is the next target. She has just gone past the park, and is heading towards the river. Her friend is a couple of minutes behind her."

"Follow, and keep an eye on them," Force suggested.

The air around him suddenly became heavy and cold. The phone connection was interrupted, and all they could hear was static. Force thought he saw a greenish shadow shimmer in front of him with a couple of slits for eyes. They seemed to burn into the very heart of his soul. The shadow shifted, and directed a sardonic smile his way.

He squinted in an effort to see better, and the creature disappeared. He sent his thoughts out into the atmosphere in an attempt to connect with it. His mind touched the monster's, and he recoiled in surprise. This was not their everyday run-of-the-mill being. It was an entity that had been created by the children themselves! He had to warn Scout. The phone line reconnected and he heard Scout shouting his name.

"Scout, I'm fine," he said into the phone. "Listen, these beings are not our normal type of creatures. They have been born out of feelings of jealousy, I think by the children that are missing."

"What?" she said into the phone.

"I know it sounds unbelievable, but they are powerful beings that are on their way to gaining the ability to become physical entities in this world. See if you can find out who, or what, Jacinta is jealous of, while I try to reconnect with the creature that just passed me. Can you keep Jacinta safe from the other one, while I try to track down this one?"

"I have more than enough magic to ward off a creature created by the emotions of children," Scout assured him confidently.

Five

Jacinta had arrived at the water's edge, and leaned her bike against a tree. She took her helmet off, and crouched down to look for tadpoles, turtles and mosquito wrigglers. A mullet fish leapt out of the water downstream, causing her to nearly fall into the water in fright.

She caught her balance and giggled at herself for being a big scaredy cat. Rummaging through her bag, she was disappointed to find she had forgotten to pack some bread. That stuff always brought the fish to the surface, if they were hungry, so she could get a better look at them. Not to worry, she was sure she could find some worms on the river bank, or some insects, that could be thrown on top of the water to encourage the fish to rise.

As she began to dig in the dirt, she heard the arrival of another bike, and spun around to greet the newcomer. The smile left Jacinta's face as her eyes rose from the black and white sneakers to the blue jeans, black and red shirt, then onto the green eyes and auburn coloured hair. Calamity had followed her, and there wasn't another soul around to provide help. Jacinta thought of two scenarios: she could make a run for it, or she could engage Calamity in conversation and try to keep it pleasant. Jacinta decided to try plan number two. "Hi, Calamity. How are you?"

"What's it to you?" the surly girl replied.

'Ok, not going well so far.' Jacinta thought she would try another tack. "Would you like to help me look for some fish and turtles?" She decided to leave out the wrigglers and tadpoles.

"Are you kidding?" Calamity scoffed. "Why would I want to do that?"

"I just thought it might be fun," mumbled Jacinta.

"You know what would be fun? It would be fun if you got back on your bike and went home, and stayed there for the rest of the day," Calamity informed her.

"Why don't you like me? I haven't done anything to you," Jacinta replied.

"Why should I like you? Come to think of it, your parents mustn't like you much either, considering how often they leave you behind."

Jacinta burst into tears, and began moving towards her bike. Calamity placed herself in front of the bike, and gave her a shove. Jacinta put her hands up in front of her face in a protective manner. "Please leave me alone. I don't want any trouble. I'll just go home and spend the rest of the day in my room."

"You should have stayed home in the first place," Calamity gloated, glad she'd managed to hurt her enemy so easily. "Think about that the next time you want to come to the river or the park to play. My friends and I should not have to have our enjoyment ruined by *you* being there. This is *our* town, not yours."

Watching the exchange, Scout was very upset by what was going on. She closed her eyes in anger, and wished really hard that she was big enough to do something to help Jacinta. When she opened her eyes, she was surprised to find that she had grown to the size of a fifteen-year-old girl. Scout felt for her wings and found they were still attached, and in full view of the humans. It was too late to worry about that now. The girls had noticed her presence, and were looking at her in astonishment.

"Who are you, and where did you come from?" Calamity demanded.

JEALOUSY MONSTERS

"My name is Scout. From what I just overheard, you are not a very nice girl at all."

"Yeah, well, that is none of your business. What's with the wings? Are you a freak or something?"

"My, but your manners need some adjusting, don't they?" Scout said. "If you must know, some of my friends and I are going to a fancy dress party. It's not something we would invite you to, but Jacinta, on the other hand, is more than welcome."

"She wouldn't be interested in going to your stupid party," Calamity said spitefully. "We are having way too much fun here, looking for fish and turtles." She waited to see if her statement would be challenged. To her surprise, it was.

"Is that right, Jacinta?" Scout asked the frightened young girl.

Jacinta thought this older girl seemed nice. She didn't feel threatened by her, even though she was a stranger. She wondered if the girl would help her get out of this situation without any strings attached. She weighed up her choices, and realised she didn't really have any. "I think a fancy-dress party might be loads of fun," Jacinta answered.

"Well, that's sorted then. Hop on your bike and we'll find you a lovely outfit that will suit your mood. Would you prefer a happy costume or a scary one?"

"A happy one please," she replied as she put on her helmet, and climbed up on to the seat.

As Jacinta pushed off and placed her feet on the pedals, she glanced back at Calamity, and saw the girl was steaming with anger. That didn't bode well, and she knew it was going to be a rough day on Monday when she arrived at school.

Scout ran beside Jacinta as she rode. The breeze whizzed through her hair and she found herself laughing with delight. Jacinta had a huge smile on her face, too. Scout told her to ride home, they needed to talk. The smile left Jacinta's face, and she wondered if she had made a huge mistake.

JEALOUSY MONSTERS

It only took a few minutes to arrive home, as it was just a few blocks up the road. She placed her bike in the rack, and her hat and helmet on the handlebars. Jacinta looked at Scout and asked, "Do you want to come inside?"

Scout looked at Jacinta, judging her mood. "Do you feel comfortable having a stranger in your home?"

Jacinta weighed her up again. "I feel that I can trust you. Come on in." Jacinta unlocked the door and they stepped into the kitchen. "We aren't going to a party, are we?" she asked.

"No. I just said that so we could get away from Calamity. She isn't very nice to you, is she?"

"No, she isn't and I don't know why. Calamity has been mean to me ever since I got here," Jacinta stated.

"How long have you been here?"

"We came here six months ago to make a fresh start," replied Jacinta.

"Why did you need a fresh start?"

"My sister, Abby, was killed in a car crash last March. My parents said they couldn't live in our old house anymore. There were too many memories of her. I miss the old place. I had friends there, and I still felt close to Abby. Now I feel like she is *there* all alone, and I am *here* all alone."

"Oh, Jacinta, I am so sorry." Scout said with feeling.

"I just wish Calamity would tell me what I did wrong, so I could fix it," Jacinta said plaintively. "I would much rather be her friend than her enemy. She won't tell me what I did, though. I guess I will spend the rest of my time here on my own."

"Won't any of the other kids be your friends?"

"No, they are all scared of Calamity, and she's told them that I'm off limits. It's okay though. She is not always at the park or the river, and there are some lovely views up in the hills. They are only an hour's walk away."

"What about your parents?"

"They spend as much time with me as their work allows. They are really busy people, but we have a lot of fun when we are able to be together."

"I meant, why don't you tell them what Calamity is doing to you?" Scout clarified.

"They have enough on their plates. I don't want to worry them with my problems."

Scout realised she was dealing with a very tough kid. Jacinta was really centred and despite the fact she had lost her sister and couldn't play with the other kids, she was actually quite a happy person. Jacinta didn't seem to be jealous about anything or anyone. Scout was beginning to think that Jacinta wasn't the child being targeted by the creatures, after all. Then she deliberated about why the trail kept leading to Jacinta, and why it was so strong around her home.

Jacinta asked Scout if she would like to come up into the hills with her, and have a look around. Scout knew she had to keep looking for the creatures. Force would be contacting her soon, and she needed to have a location of their home base ready for him. She was loathe to leave Jacinta alone. What if she ran into Calamity again? Calamity was very angry and she might really hurt Jacinta if she was given the chance.

It wouldn't hurt to accompany Jacinta to the hills. Once she had arrived safely, Scout could then continue her search for the monsters. After all, Force thought he had stumbled across their stomping grounds, which he believed were up in the hills. Scout had just finished agreeing to the suggestion, when she suddenly became small again. Jacinta blinked in confusion as Scout suddenly disappeared from view.

"Scout?" she called.

Scout flapped her wings and hovered in front of Jacinta's face. "By the way, Jacinta," she said. "I am a fairy, but you cannot tell anyone."

Jacinta would have fallen over if she hadn't already been seated on the chair. She looked at Scout with wonder. "What is it like to be a fairy?"

JEALOUSY MONSTERS

"We'll talk about it on the way to the hills." Scout had work to do, but first, she wanted to make sure Jacinta made it to her destination safely.

"Would you like to travel with me on my bike?" Jacinta offered.

Scout considered the suggestion, and decided that riding with Jacinta would conserve her energy for the flight back. "That would be lovely, Jacinta. Thank you. If I sit on your shoulder, you will be able to hear my fairy stories."

Jacinta locked the house once again, and grabbed her backpack and riding gear. Together, the pair headed north for the hills. There were no interruptions to their journey, and they made it in half the time, thanks to the bicycle. The landscape had changed from acres of cleared land, with herds of cows and tribes of goats to keep the grass down, to a more cluttered area with trees and clumps of plants.

The hills towered above them both, but were smaller than the mountains further inland.

Leaving her bicycle at the foot of the hills, Jacinta climbed swiftly and confidently. Having done this over many previous weekends, she had worked out the safest route to get to the top. The view was magnificent.

The township was laid bare for their eyes to feast upon. Blocks of greens and browns could be seen on the vegetable farming areas. Yellowish green pastures were visible on the animal farms. Farmhouses were dotted here and there.

There was so much open space below, the pair talked about how small they felt in comparison. It was a new perspective on the country for Jacinta, having come from the city with its high-rise buildings and houses practically situated on top of one another. She absolutely loved spending time in the hills.

"It really is beautiful up here. Have you shown your parents this view?"

"No," replied Jacinta. "I always come up here on my own. I never run into anyone."

JEALOUSY MONSTERS

'Except when the other two kids were poking around,' she thought. She had noticed them a couple of weeks ago. A girl and a boy about sixteen years old. He liked to wear t-shirts and jeans; she mostly wore a top and a pair of shorts, although last weekend she had a pair of jeans on too. They didn't go to her school, because she would have seen them there. It was a small school with about two hundred students ranging from prep to year twelve. She was about to mention this, when Scout began talking again.

"Thank you for showing me your special place, but I have to get back to work now. If you need me, just say my name and blow a kiss. I will hear your call and come. Don't tell anybody about me, they won't believe you. Let's just keep you and me our little secret, okay?"

"Okay. Thanks for helping me at the river, Scout."

"No worries, Jacinta. Take care."

Scout flew back to town and headed for the oak tree. She needed some more mushrooms to keep up her strength. She wondered again why the creatures had seemed to spend so much time in Jacinta's yard. If she wasn't suffering from jealousy, what could have drawn them there?

Scout was a bit concerned about leaving her alone up there all by herself. If the creatures were in the hills and were somehow using Jacinta to get to some other child, like she was beginning to suspect, she had just handed her to them on a silver platter. Force hadn't confirmed his suspicions yet, so until then, she would just have to continue in her search until she caught up with him.

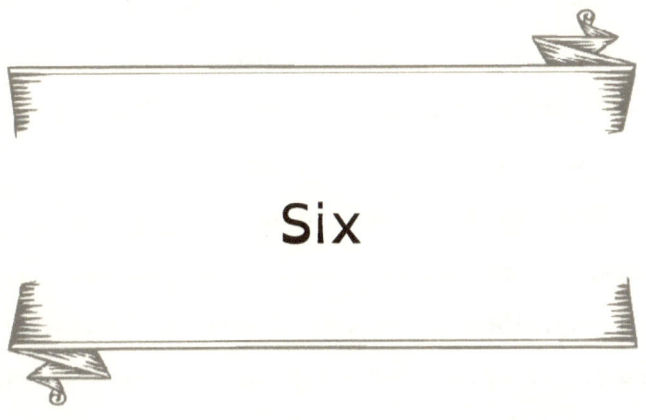

Six

Scout's phone rang and she answered it.

"Hi, Scout, where are you?" Force asked.

"Back in town. Jacinta is up in the hills. She should be safe there for a little while. I told her how to contact me if she gets in trouble and requires my assistance."

"You did what!" he screamed down the phone.

"Chill out will you. It's fine. She won't say anything. I'll tell you what happened when you get here. What is your Estimated Time of Arrival?"

"Be there in three. Don't freak out when you see an eagle. It'll be me."

"Meet me at the oak tree in the park with the monkey bars, not the one with the swings. I'll be hiding inside the hole in the trunk. You can call to me when you are in human form."

"Fine," he said and hung up.

He looked around to make sure nobody was looking, then transformed into a magnificent eagle. He spread his wings to feel their weight, then struggled to get lift. He finally got it sorted and soared high in the air. There was nothing like being a bird. The feeling of freedom when in flight, was a hard act to follow. He spotted the tree and headed for it.

The landing was soft, on a branch thick enough to hold his weight, with enough room to cater for his large wing span. Not seeing anyone within eyesight, he leapt from the branch, transforming back into a human on the way to the ground. Then wished he hadn't as his ankles and knees took the full force of the landing, and his joints hurt quite a bit.

"Ow, ow, ow," he voiced, as he hopped from one leg to the other trying to get the pain to stop. Scout peered out from the opening of the trunk, and laughed at the sight before her. She truly enjoyed working with Force and was glad they had been teamed together.

She knew she shared him with some of the other Locators but felt their relationship was stronger, as they shared a humorous outlook on life. Their joint motto was: "What was the point in living if you couldn't score a laugh?" He was so funny, her belly quite often hurt from laughter.

"Are you all right there, Hoppy?" she yelled from the safety of her tree, then realised he wouldn't be able to hear her. She projected her thoughts and was pleased when he answered her.

"I will be when the pain goes away," he replied with a grimace which only served to make the situation appear even funnier. Her laughter turned into huge guffaws. He hopped over to her position, reached in and grabbed her around the waist, trapping her wings. Her hands came down on his, and she pushed down as hard as she could, trying to squeeze her way out the top.

Now he chuckled at the jam she found herself in, and soon his pain faded away. Force carried her to a field he had seen from the sky, and sat down on the boulder. He placed her on his shoulder so he would be able to hear her speaking to him. "Have you found the hiding place for the monsters yet?" he asked her.

"No, but I am pretty sure they are not after Jacinta, even though their auras' are all over her yard and the places she visits."

"Have you noticed anyone who is extremely jealous of her?" he enquired.

"I don't know about being jealous, but there is this one girl who is really angry with her. In fact,

I would go as far as to say Calamity absolutely hates her guts."

"This Calamity is their next target then. Do you know where she is?"

"No, I don't know where she is. Why do you think she is the next target?"

He told her about the conversations he had with Michael's and Belinda's parents and their best friends. Scout nodded as his words sank in, and she realised that Calamity was behaving in a similar manner. Perhaps Calamity had spent a lot of time outside Jacinta's home, watching the interaction between daughter and parents. That would mean that Calamity had most likely already met Ruby and Lucas, and they had fed on her jealousy, as she had stood at the window looking in.

Everything started to make sense to Scout. She began to understand the reason why the swirls were around Jacinta, even though she felt happy, if a little sad. There was not an angry or jealous bone in Jacinta's body, like the monsters required, but *Calamity* had been hanging around.

However, Scout couldn't work out why she was having so much trouble locating the monsters.

Perhaps it was because they were not yet strong enough to survive on their own. They still needed the power that the children supplied, to materialise in this world. She also pondered why the location of the missing children had not been found yet. The entities must be holding them somewhere, feeding off their emotions until they could burst into life.

Scout voiced all of her thoughts to Force, and asked him how she was supposed to locate something that didn't really exist yet. He told her that she couldn't. For this case, they would need to switch positions. He would need to do the locating by fixing onto Calamity's mind, and she would need to do the capturing with her fairy magic.

Scout was both excited and terrified by his proposition. Excited, because she would finally be able to stay on a mission from start to finish, and witness the capturing of a creature. She usually had to leave once the Gatherer was on the trail, to find the location of the next threat. Yet she was terrified that she might screw it up, and the child they were trying to save now would be in the same predicament as her last child had been, anguished and withdrawn.

Force, on the other hand, was happy to be able to let Scout feel what it was like to be the hero for once. He knew she was satisfied with her role in the capturing of creatures. He also knew that she felt her role was nothing special compared to his. She didn't understand the value of her incredible gift, of being able to locate the creatures. He sent his spirit out and touched on a few minds before finding the one he was looking for. "I found her," he said. "She is at the park with her friends."

"Let's go," Scout called, flapping her wings.

"Hold on a minute, how did the kid find out you were a fairy?"

"I got really angry when Calamity was bullying Jacinta, and I wished I was big enough to protect her. Next thing I knew, I was, but it didn't last," Scout said.

"Are you kidding me?"

"Nope, real deal."

"Does Calamity know you are a fairy?" he asked. When she shook her head in reply, he said, "Hmmm, time to make myself small I think," and transformed himself into a fairy. "We can travel together and stay hidden while we watch Calamity's interaction with her friends."

Seven

They arrived at the other park, and saw three of Calamity's friends, but no Calamity. Force and Scout landed in a tree and watched with confusion.

"Where is Calamity?" enquired Scout.

"I don't know. I can feel her presence and hear her thoughts as clear as day, but I can't see her."

"Shouldn't we be looking for her?" Scout asked him.

"And risk being spotted by them?" he answered, pointing to the children on the swings. "She is here somewhere, and while she is projecting a lot of anger, she is not in any danger from anyone other than herself."

"We need to find her," Scout said anxiously.

"Scout, we know that it is likely that the next child, probably Calamity, will be taken in the next couple of days. Calamity is twelve. So if it is her that the creatures are after, she will be taken sometime today being the twelfth of the month.

"The other children did not disappear until after three o'clock in the afternoon. Therefore, we have at least five and a half hours to try to figure out how the monsters are making the children disappear, and where their base is located. Can you feel the creatures with your magic?"

Scout closed her eyes and concentrated, while Force wondered once again why he continued to call the creatures 'monsters' when conversing with Scout. He found it hard enough to remember to change his eye colour when around others, let alone that the Queen and the Guardians would not approve of his using the word 'monsters'.

Shaking his head he waited to see what Scout had discovered. They were still in the area but very faint. She could tell they weren't with Calamity and she thought she could sense the missing children. She just couldn't see where they were. Scout began to calm as she realised Calamity was not in any immediate danger. She wouldn't be of much use if she allowed herself to get into a tizzy.

"Were any of them taken on a Saturday?" she asked him.

He thought about it and came to the realisation that the other children were all taken on school days. He didn't want her to become more agitated so he just shrugged his shoulders, but now he felt a greater sense of urgency within himself.

The kids in the park were having a blast. Jeremy was blonde with a dark grey t-shirt, aqua coloured shorts, and dark grey and aqua coloured joggers. At that particular moment, he was running around pretending he was an aeroplane, after having pushed the girls on the swings.

The girls were wearing the same style dresses but in different colours. Breanna had long brown hair that was tied back in a ponytail. Her sleeveless, bright yellow dress fell to her knees. She had grey sneakers with white ankle socks. Hannah had blonde, curly hair that was tied up in pigtails. Her dress was white with red roses and green leaves printed all over it. She wore red stockings with red shoes that had white across the toe area and a gold heart buckle that clasped across the front of her ankle.

The children were certainly enjoying their freedom, having been released from their duties of helping their parents at the bake sale.

Scout noticed the leaves in the tree on the other side of the park swish. There was no breeze, so she elbowed Force in the ribs and pointed in the tree's direction. He was about to ask her what she was going on about when he saw the leaves rustle, too. His eyes closed to a squint as he thought about flying over for a closer look, when Calamity's face appeared between the branches.

She was up in the tree watching her friends' antics, which made them wonder how long she had been there, and why she was there in the first place.

"What do you think she is doing, hiding in the tree?" Scout asked.

"I don't know. She's a strange one, isn't she!" he exclaimed.

They watched the girls swinging back and forth, while Jeremy scurried around with his arms still held out to the side. Calamity shifted on the branch, which cracked loudly and deposited her on the ground, screaming in pain. She landed right on her bottom before flipping over on to her tummy.

"Calamity?" Jeremy asked as he raced over to her. The girls jumped off the swings in mid-flight and joined him. "Where do you hurt?"

"My butt is broken!" she screamed.

"You can't break your butt, there are no bones in there," Hannah told her.

"Of course there are! They're broken! I can feel them!" Calamity yelled in response.

"Would you like me to rub it for you?" Breanna asked.

"No, I don't want you to rub it for me. Go and get the doctor right now!" Calamity ordered her friends. All three stood up to leave to get help, but discovered they didn't need to go anywhere. Force had flown to the ground and transformed himself back into his normal state. None of the kids seemed frightened by his sudden appearance. In fact they seemed mighty pleased to see him.

"What seems to be the trouble here?" Force asked.

"Calamity fell out of the tree and broke her butt," Jeremy said laughing.

"Don't you laugh at me, a-hole!"

"I can't even see your a-hole, but I am sure it is broken too," Jeremy said now in full hysterics.

"That's not what I meant and you know it," Calamity sobbed.

"How about you kids go play while I take a look at Calamity," Force suggested.

"Who are you?" asked Hannah.

"My name is Force."

"What sort of a name is that?" Breanna asked him.

"That would be my last name and what most people call me," he replied.

"Are you a doctor?" Calamity asked.

"Sure," he replied.

The kids shrugged their shoulders and said they had to check in with their parents at the bake sale, anyway.

"You be okay?" Hannah asked Calamity.

"Of course not. I am lying on the ground broken, but you go off and help your mothers. I thought you were supposed to have been there an hour and a half ago."

"They decided we were more hindrance than help, and sent us away again," Breanna stated unhappily.

"We have to check in at ten," Jeremy said.

"It is ten minutes to ten now," Force said consulting his watch.

"Better go then," Jeremy said to the girls.

Force watched the kids walk away then turned his attention to Calamity. "Ok, Calamity, let's see what you have done."

"I didn't do anything. The branch broke and threw me down here."

"I see. Can you stand?"

She tried to get to her feet but the pain was too intense, "No," she sobbed.

He placed his hand on her bottom and sent out a wave of spirit with her screaming at him to get his hands off her. "Can you get up now?"

She spun over on to her bottom and gave him a piece of her mind.

"Yep, I'll take that as a 'yes'," he insisted.

She stopped yammering at him and discovered she was sitting on the thing that had caused her no measure of pain, minutes ago. "How did you do that?" she demanded, getting to her feet.

"Magic," he replied.

"No, seriously, how did you do that?"

"Like I said, magic."

He got to his feet and walked towards the road. Calamity quickly followed, demanding an explanation for her miraculous recovery. He refused to answer her and kept walking. "Can you walk with me to Donovan's place?" she asked him.

He stopped and looked at her. "Why?"

"I don't know. I would just like some company."

"Aren't you worried I might be a bad person? I did just touch your bottom after all."

"Yes, you did, and now it doesn't hurt anymore. Besides, you got up and walked away once I was better. If you were a bad person, I would be screaming for my life now, wouldn't I?"

"Fine. You aren't going to talk my ear off are you?"

"No. I'll be quiet as a mouse."

Eight

He melded with her mind to check the truth of that statement. She would be quiet for about two minutes, and then would talk his ear off the whole way. Fantastic. 'This is the best opportunity ever,' he thought. 'Absolutely perfect.'

Force looked at the tree where Scout was hiding, and found her flicking her hands at him in a gesture to get going. Before he turned away, she blew him a kiss and he suddenly felt his cheeks blush. He wished that Calamity would begin talking now, but knew it would still be another one hundred and ten seconds before her mouth would open. Which left him one hundred and ten seconds to think about his reaction to Scout's actions.

They had been working together for the past five years. She was fun to work with, and beautiful to look at. She had a humorous outlook on life just like him, and a passion for helping children who were being targeted by the nastiest of creatures. She was dedicated to her job, and a delight to work with.

He imagined what it would be like to kiss her properly. He pictured himself small and wrapping his arms around her waist, pulling her close until their lips touched. His breathing quickened and he felt that he would enjoy the experience of kissing her for real.

"You okay there, Force?"

"What?"

"Are you all right? You were breathing a bit hard. I guess you are too old to walk this far. Thought you were younger than my mum, though. Maybe you sit around too much in that job of yours, and don't get enough exercise. Are you one of those doctors who sits at your desk and have the patients come to you, or one of those doctors who run around all the time in the hospitals, kissing the nurses in the closets?"

"I am fine and I get plenty of exercise," he said showing her the muscles in his arms.

"That doesn't mean you are fit," she informed him.

"No, it doesn't," he agreed.

"Are you going to die if you keep walking with me?"

"No, I won't die if I walk with you to Donovan's." She didn't seem convinced but kept walking anyway. Force could see a house off to the left in the distance. "Is that where we are going?"

"Nah, that's the Jenkins'. Donovan lives further along with his twin brother, William."

"Why are you going to Donovan and William's place anyway?"

"Jacinta has gone off to some dumb party with some older chick in a costume, and the others have gone to the bake sale."

"What are you planning on doing at the boys' place?"

"They have pony club later in the day so they will be at the stables getting the horses ready. I thought I could hang out with them until their lesson starts, and pat the horses."

"That sounds nice, what about your parents?"

"What about them?" Calamity pouted.

"How come you aren't spending time with them? It is the weekend."

"Mum's busy and Dad left when I was two."

"Oh, I'm sorry."

"Yeah, well, you don't need to be. I'm not. There are a few horses over there running around," she said pointing in their direction.

Force looked over the fence and saw the three palominos galloping around the paddock. There were two big horses and one smaller horse, and he made the assumption they were parents and foal. They were simply beautiful. Their coats were glossy and their muscles rippled as they moved. Their manes flowed freely in the breeze, and they whinnied in a happy sounding way.

He noticed something a little further up the hill and morphed his eyes into those of an eagle so he could get a better look. Sitting in the middle of the paddock was a tin sheet curved into a semicircle. Standing on top of it were three baby goats. They were so cute.

The first was brown and white, the second was pure white and the third was fully black. He watched them for a few minutes, jumping down and then climbing up again, sometimes using each other as a jumping post. He chuckled at their antics, and brought attention to himself. Calamity's gasp of breath, told him she had caught sight of his eyes, before he had changed them back to brown.

"Ummmmmmmm," she hummed.

"Calamity, are you okay?"

When she didn't answer him, he bent down and looked at her, eye level to eye level. "Calamity?"

"Oh, I thought your eyes were different than they are, and they scared me," she whispered to him.

"What did they look like?" he questioned her.

"They were really creepy. Kind of a yellowish orange colour and your blacks looked like thin slits."

"Really? It must have been the way the sunlight was hitting my face."

Calamity giggled. "The sunlight can't hit your face. It's light."

"It is just a figure of speech."

"Ha, ha, ha. You are really funny, Mr. Force."

"Just Force."

"Okay," she said giggling harder, "You are really funny, just Force."

"Why do I have to deal with children?" he muttered to himself.

They had arrived at the gate to the Jenkins' place but kept walking. It was another five hundred metres past the rise before they would reach the gate to William and Donovan's home. Calamity seemed to be feeling quite content and safe. Force thought about what he had learned so far about Calamity.

She was a little fireball when interacting with her friends. Of course, that had nothing to do with her bright, auburn coloured hair. He believed it had more to do with the environment she was growing up in, than the genes she had inherited. She didn't understand the boundary between adult and child, and was quite familiar and disrespectful when conversing with him.

He thought it was time to bring up Jacinta and see where the conversation and her mood led. "You said earlier that Jacinta was off to a party with some girl."

"Yeah, so?"

"How come you didn't go with her?"

"I wasn't invited and wouldn't go with that brat anyway."

"You're not friends then?"

"No, why would I be friends with an awful girl like her?"

"How is she awful?"

"She just is." Calamity began snapping her answers at him. She didn't want to discuss Jacinta with him, or anyone else. She hated her so much it was painful. Her hands had bunched into fists and her eyes had become shadowed with hatred.

Force watched the reaction with interest. He noticed the almost immediate tensing of the young girl beside him, and the change in her tone of voice. This was a girl with some serious issues, and he realised just how powerful and dangerous this emotion was to humans. He also began to understand how an evil entity could be born, as a result of such a powerfully negative feeling.

"Come on, Calamity. It's just us two," he said crossing his fingers. He knew full well, that Scout had caught up to them while Calamity wasn't looking, and had placed herself in the pocket of his pants. "What's up with Jacinta?"

"I just don't like her. Her Mum and Dad dote on her. They spend time with her doing things she likes and when they are at work, she is allowed to go wherever she wants. How is that fair?"

"Why isn't it fair?" he asked her gently.

"Because my Mum yells at me all the time, even when I do what she tells me to do. She always tells me to go to my room, and will never play games with me or anything. My Dad loved me so much he didn't even take me with him when he left. He just left me at home with *her*. How is that fair?"

She threw herself at him, wrapping her arms around his waist and burying her head into his chest as she sobbed. He stood for a few seconds before he placed his hands on her back and hugged her back. Force let her cry and cry and cry, until she was all cried out.

When she came up for air, he pushed the hair out of her eyes, and grabbed the handkerchief from the other pocket to the one Scout was in, and wiped her tears. She refused to look him in the eyes, preferring to keep them facing the ground. Calamity turned around and walked towards the boys' place. Force followed.

Scout felt a jolt as she picked up on the creatures' life threads. She tugged on the material of Force's pants but he never felt it, so she tickled his leg through the material making up the pocket. His hand reacted automatically and swiped at the tickle.

He called out her name and melded his mind with hers. Calamity spun around thinking he had been calling out to her.

His eyes had changed colour again as his mind connected with Scout's. Calamity screamed with fear, and ran for Donovan's place.

Force was relieved to discover Scout wasn't hurt, and was interested to see that the creatures had resurfaced. He was also pleased to see that Scout had narrowed down the location of the creatures' hideout, to somewhere up in the mountains. Then he became concerned that they might run into Jacinta.

He stretched his mind further and saw that Jacinta was making her way back into town. She seemed a little distressed but he was not concerned that it might have something to do with the creatures. He disengaged his mind from Scout and Jacinta, to discover Calamity was gone.

He spun in a circle, but couldn't see her figure anywhere. He sent his thought waves across the landscape and found her entering the doors to the stables. Wow, he had made a mess of this job, and he had the gall to rip it up Scout for allowing Jacinta to know of her existence.

He had some work to do in securing Calamity's trust and secrecy. Force ran until he had arrived within twenty metres of the stables. Then he

JEALOUSY MONSTERS

slowed to a leisurely walk and entered the
stable, just as Calamity had finished telling her
friends her story, of the man who had healed
her broken butt, and had scary, devil eyes.

Nine

Donovan, William, their pony club friend Justine, and Calamity spun around as Force walked through the doorway to the stables.

Calamity cringed and hid behind her friends in fear. The two boys and Justine were dressed in their riding gear consisting of a cream, long-sleeved shirt, black jacket, black jodhpurs and riding boots. The two boys were identical in appearance with bald heads and brilliant blue eyes. Justine was a pretty girl, with brown skin, wavy brown hair with gold highlights and dark brown eyes. Force sauntered up to the nearest horse and said, "What's up?"

The boys burst into laughter and William said, "Yeah, he's real scary, Calamity."

Donovan peered into Force's face and remarked, "His eyes are as brown as Justine's and hers are pretty dark. How did you ever think they were yellow?"

"He's probably got his contacts back in," she said angrily. Calamity didn't like to be made fun of. She was the one that usually poked fun at everyone else.

"I don't wear contacts," Force told them with a smile, "but you are welcome to have a closer look."

"Nah, it's all good man," William said. "We know what she's like when she gets a bee in her bonnet."

"Oh, for goodness sake, what are you doing here? I don't need you anymore. Go away," Calamity said to Force.

"See what I mean?" William said. "She can be quite rude."

"I'll just go home and do my own thing. See you later," Calamity told her friends.

"Don't be silly, Calamity. We love having you here, and so do the horses. I am sure Mister has somewhere he needs to be," Justine said.

"Nope, there is nowhere I have to be or anything I need to be doing. Actually, I wouldn't mind catching up with a couple of kids if you know where they might be hanging out. Their names are Ruby and Lucas."

"Don't know them," the three friends stated. Force had been watching Calamity when he spoke their names and saw her eyes grow big and her throat move as she swallowed. "What about you, Calamity? Do you know them?"

"No, never met them before in my life," she lied.

JEALOUSY MONSTERS

"Oh, well, guess I will ask around when I check out the bake sale. I will probably go and get some lunch later. Are you kids going?"

"Yeah, after pony club," they chorused.

The kids grabbed the brushes and began grooming the horses. Justine braided the manes as the boys took care of their coats. They got the blankets, bridles, saddles and stirrups ready. The horses looked on and nodded their heads as if they were giving the children their approval.

Force watched their preparations with admiration. There was not an adult in sight and the children just got on with the job in a very professional manner. He was often surprised by their knowledge and dedication. They took such care when dealing with the animals, treating them with the respect they deserved.

William opened the gate to lead his horse, Spirit, out of the stall so he had more room to prep him for riding, just as Ruby's and Lucas' essences arrived. The horses became skittish, and Spirit bolted as Lucas slapped him on the rump. He ran straight for the opening to the paddock, and didn't stop when he felt the rays of the sun stroke his head and back.

"Bloody hell!" William yelled as he took off after the horse.

"Oh, my God!" Justine screamed as she followed.

Donovan didn't say a word. He checked that the other horses were secure, and tried to calm them, before running after Spirit. Force had a dilemma. He could feel the difference in the air, and could hear the thoughts of the creatures that had not had the power to materialise fully. They wanted Calamity alone and it was his job to protect her, but they had scared Spirit, and the kids had now put themselves in a dangerous situation.

He knew that if they had just left the horse alone, it would have calmed down and remained safe out in the paddock. They were not going to give it a chance to calm down. They were going to scare it more by running after it and trying to catch it. If he didn't go after the kids, one of them might become seriously hurt. If he did go after them, Calamity would probably end up with the other missing children.

"Scout, will your magic hold the creatures in their current form?" he asked her.

"No," she answered.

Calamity would just have to go with them. He grabbed her by the arm and pulled her towards the door. She kicked and screamed and dragged her feet behind her.

"For goodness sake, your friends are in trouble!" he shouted at her.

"I don't care. I am scared of horses running wild when they are not behind a fence!" she screamed.

"Too bad. It's about time you thought of someone other than yourself."

He kept dragging her, until she realised she was going to end up with broken shoes, or an arm that was pulled out of its shoulder socket. She stopped fighting him and began running with him. Adrenalin pumped through her veins, heightening her senses.

The air smelled of grass and horse manure. The breeze played with her hair as she ran, gently brushing her skin. It reminded her of a time when her mother used to play with her hair at bedtime while telling her fairy-tale stories.

That, of course, was before her father had left. Wow, she couldn't believe she had forgotten that. There was actually a time when her mother had shown her affection. Suddenly, she felt very lonely and sad that she had chased her father away, and made her mother hate her. Her lungs burned with the effort of dragging the air down into their depths, and her sides began to hurt.

It had been a long time since she had gone for a run, and she realised she was more out of shape than the old man running beside her. She wondered how old he was, probably twenty-five or six. Her mum was thirty-three, and she thought he looked a bit younger than that.

Calamity's friends were just ahead of her, doubled over trying to catch their breath. Force and Calamity caught up with them, and she was surprised to see that he showed no sign of the physical effort he had just put in. She, on the other hand, was sucking in the air in a loud and unladylike fashion.

"Where . . . is . . . the . . . horse?" she asked no-one in particular.

"Way over there," William replied, pointing to the north.

"Oh," replied Calamity. "Should we keep going?"

"No, he will come to us if we don't jump around and scare him again," Donovan said importantly.

"How do you know that?" asked Calamity.

"Because he does this all the time," said William laughing.

"He what?" asked Calamity. "Then why did we just run after him?"

"For fun," replied Donovan. "Running after Spirit is so much more fun than just running after each other."

"Yeah, we do that every lunch time at school. We love it when Spirit makes us chase him. Look how happy he is," Justine said.

The children looked at him off in the distance, happily grazing. Force knew his happiness had nothing to do with the chase. He was just happy to be outside and not cooped up in the enclosed confines of the stables. His mouth tugged at the clumps of grass and chewed merrily.

"Yes, he looks very happy," Force agreed. "What do we do now?"

"Now we play truth or dare," Donovan announced.

"I don't think so," Force stated. "Don't you have pony club? I can wait with Spirit and bring him back when he is ready."

"He won't come to you. Besides, our teacher is used to us being late due to Spirit's escapades," William said.

"So why do you let him out of his stall beforehand?" Force questioned.

"I don't know. Because it's fun?" Donovan responded.

"Maybe you don't really like pony club?" Force asked them.

"Yeah, not really," the children replied.

"Have you told your parents how you feel?"

"No pony club, no horses. Don't really have a choice," Justine said.

"It's not so bad. They teach us how to look after our horses which is pretty important," William told him.

"I see," Force replied.

"Truth or Dare, Mister?" asked Donovan.

"Neither."

"You can't say 'neither'," Justine informed him. "If you don't choose one, then we automatically ask you a question and you have to tell the truth."

"Oh, my goodness, my mother," Calamity said with horror.

They all followed her eyes and saw her mother's car flying down the road. They looked at one another knowingly. Calamity was never going to beat her mother home, and she was going to be in so much trouble. Calamity ran as fast as she could towards home.

"Good luck, Calamity."

"See you at school on Monday."

"Sorry kids, I've got to go too. Are you going to be okay with Spirit?"

"Of course we are," Donovan told him. "We do this every Saturday, remember?"

"Exactly," said Force shaking his head.

"What are you kids doing?" called Mrs. Humphries from the stables.

"Getting ready for pony club," yelled William.

"You idiots," she replied. "I told you last week that there would be no pony club this week because of the bake sale."

Ten

Force caught up to Calamity and tried to talk to her. She was in no mood to talk, and was physically incapable of speaking with the effort she was putting in to beat her mother home. So they ran together in silence.

They started running the same way they had followed Spirit, but then Calamity suddenly made a break to the right. She headed towards the hills and he assumed she was taking a short cut. For some reason, he didn't feel like tapping into her mind. He felt he needed to give her some privacy at the moment.

It never occurred to him to transform himself into some woodsy creature. Unfortunately, some of the local women had spotted a man chasing Calamity through the paddock. It was quite easy to identify her, as she was the only person in town with that particular shade of hair colour.

They kept calling Calamity's mum until she arrived home and picked up the phone. Already in a bad mood, Loretta stormed out of the house to face the man that threatened her baby's safety. She didn't bother removing her high heeled sandals, or change out of her strapless dress. Her daughter was in danger and needed her right away.

She hurried down the stairs and took off in the direction indicated by her neighbours. She had reached the border of her property when she saw her daughter appear over the hill, followed by a tall, athletic looking man.

"Run, Calamity!" she screamed.

"What?" Calamity replied as she stumbled with confusion caused by her mother's words. Calamity looked over her shoulder and saw Force still running behind her. "It's not what you think, Mother."

"Get away from her!" Loretta yelled at Force, as she pulled the top of her dress down for a couple of seconds, and flashed her breasts at him. Calamity reached her mother and placed her hands on her mother's arms.

"He is a friend," Calamity said.

"Don't be ridiculous. He is too old to be a friend. He is a perv and has no business talking to you."

"No, you are wrong," Calamity said, as Force recovered from his tumble caused by her mother's distraction tactics. "He is a doctor. I fell out of a tree and he made sure I was okay."

"A doctor, really?" she said to him.

Force pulled out his wallet, found the business card with Dr. Wade Force on it and handed it to Loretta. She looked at it with astonishment. "I am so sorry for the assumptions I made. Please forgive me for flashing you. I am so embarrassed."

"Don't worry about it. I understand how frightening it must have looked, with me running after your daughter. Especially after the reports of the missing children. I totally understand your needing to distract me, and let me tell you, it was extremely effective," he said with a smile.

She looked at him properly for the first time and noticed how handsome he was. She fixed up her pony tail and ran her hands over her dress, smoothing out the wrinkles. He could feel the attraction pouring from her veins and felt it was time to leave. Now that her mum was feeling a bit happier, he hoped that Calamity wouldn't be in as much trouble as she might have been a few minutes earlier.

"I'm sorry, Mrs. . . ."

"Loretta. You can call me Loretta."

"Loretta, I have to go. Dr. Warren is sick and he has asked me to take a look at a couple of his patients before I leave town. I am sorry I frightened you. Your daughter is fine. Surprisingly, she didn't even suffer a scrape or bruise." Because, of course, he had healed them when he touched her at the park. "See you, little miss. Take care of yourself and stay out of the trees."

"Would you like to have dinner with me tonight?" Loretta asked him hopefully.

"I would love to, but I don't think my wife would approve," he said with a serious face.

"What a shame. For me. I meant what a shame for me."

"Take care, both of you."

Force left and hoped Loretta wouldn't be too hard on Calamity. Loretta was very attractive and he had been very tempted to have dinner with her. Unfortunately, in his line of work, relationships never lasted and the lady always got hurt. Loretta seemed to have enough hurt in her life already, without him adding to it. He gently nudged her mind as he left and discovered an aching hole where Calamity's dad had been.

It seems Calamity's dad had gotten mixed up in a drug ring trying to make some extra money to buy her a Christmas present, and had gotten himself killed. Loretta had wrongly thought it was better that Calamity thought her dad had run out on them, rather than getting killed for doing something illegal. Hopefully, Calamity would learn the truth one day, and know that her dad loved her very much after all.

Perhaps when the creatures were vanquished, he could help Loretta see that Calamity would be better off knowing who her father really was; a man who had simply made the wrong choice because of the love he had for his daughter.

Eleven

Calamity began to walk home but was stopped by her angry mother.

"Just a minute, young lady. Come back here."

Loretta waited for her daughter to stand where she pointed, before continuing the lecture. "Where have you been and what have you been doing? You were supposed to stay home today! I hope you have tidied your room."

"I wanted to pet the horses so I went over to Will and Donovan's place."

"And when were you at the park?"

"Before I went over to Will's," Calamity admitted.

"Dammit, Calamity, I have to earn a living. I'm not smart and I don't have any talents. I need you to help out around the place while I go over to Callahan's to do my modelling jobs."

"I'm sorry, Mother. I'll tidy my room as soon as we get home."

"You bet your bottom you will," Loretta said in agreement. "You know there is someone out there stealing children. That man, the doctor, could have been the person taking them, and I would not have even known where to start looking for you. How could you be so inconsiderate? Why can't you just do what you are told?"

They walked back to the house together. Loretta with head held high, even though the heels of her sandals could bury themselves in the dirt and send her flying at any moment.

JEALOUSY MONSTERS

Calamity wandered slowly, with head down and tears welling in her eyes. It was so much better when she didn't get caught.

Why was her mum home so early anyway? She usually had a few hours to do as she wanted, before she ran home to carry out the instructions her mother had given her. She wanted to ask her mum but was too frightened. They had walked up the stairs and she waited for her mother to unlock the door, but it was already unlocked.

Her mum must have been pretty upset earlier to have not locked up when she left. Loretta had always left the house unlocked until a couple of months ago. Now all of a sudden, every time she went somewhere for any length of time, even if Calamity was left at home, she locked the house up tight, windows and all.

Luckily for Calamity, she was able to open the windows in her room from the inside, and used them to climb out onto the veranda, and then down the stairs to freedom. She always made sure to close them behind her, and used an iron bar to pry them open again when she got home. So far, her mother hadn't noticed the bits of missing paint and the indentation marks in the wood.

Entering the house, she went to walk down the hallway to her room, when her mum pulled her up. "On second thoughts, how about you help me put Sally's wedding invitations in their envelopes. There are only two hundred, so it shouldn't take longer than an hour between the two of us."

"Yes, Mother," Calamity grumbled.

"And lose the attitude or I'll make you do them on your own."

Calamity kept her mouth shut for once, and was rewarded by sharing the work with her mother. She shouldn't have complained because she had been wanting to spend some time with her mother for ages, and here they were, together.

Calamity was young though, and wanted the time to be spent doing things *she* wanted to do, rather than enjoying the fact that she had her mother all to herself. It really shouldn't have mattered what they were doing, but it did.

Calamity was feeling resentful, and her mother was filled with disappointment at the emotion that was displayed all over Calamity's face. She could see that her daughter was unhappy, but didn't know what else she could do to change that fact. She was about to ask her, when Calamity started up a conversation. Loretta decided to see where it would lead, and hoped it would give her an insight into where her daughter's thoughts were currently taking her.

"How did the photo shoot go this morning?"

"It was cancelled, Honey. I did get to see the new clothing line though. This dress will be on the shelves in a couple of weeks," she said pointing to the outfit she was wearing.

"Is that how they paid you?"

"Yeah, I'm afraid so. I only get paid money when the shoots go ahead."

"Why was it cancelled?"

"The photographer is sick. It's been rescheduled for next Saturday. Is that going to be a problem?"

"We were going to spend the day together on Saturday to celebrate my birthday, seeing though it falls on a school day."

"I know honey, but we kind of need the money. I promise you will have my undivided attention for the rest of the day once the shoot is over."

"Fine, you can work it."

"Thanks."

They continued stuffing envelopes in silence for the next fifteen minutes. The Smiths, the Humphries, the Jones's, the Tillies. Wait a minute. That was Jacinta's last name. "Mum, are Jacinta's parents invited to Sally's wedding?"

"Let me see. Yes, they all are," her mum confirmed.

"God, dammit," Calamity grumbled.

"I beg your pardon?"

"Sorry, Mother."

"Do you have a problem with the Tillies?"

"No, Mother."

"It didn't sound like that to me. What happened?"

"Nothing. I don't have a problem with the Tillies," Calamity said. '*I just have a problem with Jacinta,*' she thought.

"Why won't you talk to me?" her mum asked.

"We *are* talking," Calamity replied.

Loretta felt herself becoming upset. She could continue trying to connect with her daughter and watch her become even more miserable, or she could let her go to clean her room. She decided to send her to her room.

"Go and do your room, Calamity. I can finish this up on my own."

Calamity looked at her mum with angry, upset eyes. Once again, her mother was sending her away and didn't want to spend time with her. She didn't know why she bothered wishing to be closer to her mother. She always ended up feeling upset and irritated at the end of their sessions, and wished she had never sat with her in the first place.

Calamity got up and walked down the hallway in a huff. She opened the door to her room and slammed it closed, locking it behind her. Loretta heard the click of the lock, and told herself once again, that she would have to remove the locking mechanism of Calamity's door. She was sick of Calamity locking her out, physically and emotionally.

Loretta got up and went through the kitchen and out the back door. She walked down the stairs, unlocked, and entered the shed. Time to find the screwdrivers and fix the lock, once and for all.

Calamity threw herself on the bed and kicked her legs while she screamed into her pillow. That was it. She needed to find a way to make her life better. Perhaps she should leave, too.

Her mother would be fine without her. In fact, she would probably be a lot happier without her around. Where to go, though? She heard a tapping sound and wondered what her mother was doing. She lifted her head from the pillow and saw her friends tapping on the glass of the window.

Twelve

Calamity jumped off the bed and threw her windows open. Ruby and Lucas climbed inside. They sat on her bed and invited her to join them. She preferred to sit in the armchair beside her bedside table, so she could see them better.

Lucas was tall and fair skinned. He had black hair with reddish-brown highlights throughout his fringe that was brushed into a long prickle cut. His smile was friendly and his eyes twinkled like emeralds. He wore a white t-shirt with dark green zigzags emblazoned across the front, dark blue jeans and a pair of navy coloured thongs on his feet.

Ruby was a few inches shorter with brunette hair placed in two low pigtails. Her brown eyes were mischievous and her smile held the hint of slyness. She had a black crop top that was covered by a short-sleeved shirt in a sheer material that had been dyed a cream colour. She wore grey jeans and beige coloured, flat-strappy sandals.

"What are you guys doing here?" Calamity asked with a smile.

"Thought you might need a friend," Ruby said, smiling in return.

"What are you up to?" Lucas asked, already knowing what had been on her mind.

"Trying to think of somewhere else I could live. I don't want to live here anymore."

"Why not? Your mother seems to care for you a lot," Ruby remarked.

"Are you kidding? She yells at me all the time, and she gets upset when we spend any time together. Then she ends up telling me to go to my room. Why, just now, she is sitting in the living room finishing a job she asked me to help her with."

"No, she's not," said Lucas. "She's gone to the shed to find some screwdrivers to take the lock off your door."

"She's what?"

"You heard me."

"Come on, let's go," Calamity said, standing up from her chair and tugging at the teenagers' arms to join her.

"Not yet," Ruby said.

"We should wait until she nearly gets the lock off, then jump out the window. It would do her good to see you running away, and might make her treat you better when you come home," Lucas said.

"She will be madder than ever," Calamity stated.

"No, she won't," said Ruby. "She will be so worried when she sees you leave, she will cover you in hugs and kisses when you show up safe and sound in a few hours' time."

"Do you really think so?" Calamity asked, full of hope.

"You bet, Short Strap," Lucas replied cunningly.

"So, what should we do in the meantime?"

"How about you grab your school bag, and pack it with a few supplies. You know, make it look like you have left home, and give your mum a fright. Then, just before nightfall, we'll bring you home and your mum will open her arms to you," Lucas suggested.

"Really?" Calamity squeaked. She grabbed her bag from the floor in the corner, and threw the doors to her wardrobe open. She flicked through the outfits her mum had placed neatly on hangers, and found her favourites. She pulled them out of the wardrobe, tossed the hangers on the floor, and stuffed the tops, shorts and jeans in her bag. She went to her drawers and pulled out some undies, hair brush, hair ties and her favourite bangles.

Ruby had walked over to the other corner of the room and peered at her stuffed toy collection. She picked up the teddy bears, unicorns and bunny rabbits with disgust and threw them on the floor. Calamity turned and saw her toys lying on the floor, and raced over to pick them up.

"What are you doing?" she cried in alarm.

They were her greatest source of comfort. She picked up the closest bear, a gorgeous little pink thing of fluff, with big, black eyes and a cute, black, button nose. She carefully placed it in her bag.

Ruby reminded her she was supposed to be running away and upsetting her mum as much as possible. Only then would her return be all the sweeter. Calamity disliked her mum at present, but didn't despise her. She didn't want to hurt her mother, or make her upset by leaving behind a messy room.

Calamity was quite good at keeping her room tidy. Her mother's idea of Calamity cleaning her room, involved dusting the knick-knacks that lined the flat surfaces in her room, and giving the floor a quick vacuum. Ensuring the bed was made and the pillow was fluffed up. The curtains drawn back so the sunlight could get into the room to kill the nasties. The windows opened to let in the fresh air and remove the stale air. The door on the wardrobe closed, so, too, the drawers of the tallboy. Her jewellery tucked safely into her jewellery box, and the little bit of makeup her mother allowed her to have, placed neatly on top of her dressing table.

The mirror must be wiped over and streak free. Her book collection dust free and lined up neatly in alphabetical order, first by author and then by title. There was no way she could leave her things strewn all over the room. Especially something she cared about as much as her toy collection.

Calamity picked up her toys and placed them carefully back in their correct positions. She had no problem leaving her hangers on the floor, but she had to draw a line at her personal stuff, and she let the teenagers know it. They simply shrugged their shoulders and continued their investigation of her possessions. Calamity was a bit disturbed to see Lucas going through her underwear drawer, and told him she had already gotten what she needed from there. He snickered and slammed the drawer shut, moving on to the next.

Ruby picked up a photo of Calamity's dad and looked at it carefully. He shared the same intense blue eyes with his daughter. It was like looking into hers, except his were full of love and laughter, and hers were full of jealousy and despair. Where her hair was auburn red, his was chestnut brown. His skin was tanned from working the land, whereas hers was tanned from sneaking out and playing without permission.

It was clear that she got her femininity from her mother. Her father had been a very masculine creature before his demise, and her mother was incredibly beautiful. Way too beautiful to be a woman on the land, which is why she earned enough money from modelling, to survive in the country without the farm providing an income.

The main reason Loretta stayed, was to feel close to her dead husband, and to give Calamity the opportunity to grow up with nature. She didn't want Calamity to become consumed by the city and its self-obsessed teenagers. She had hoped to keep Calamity innocent of such things for as long as possible.

Too bad she felt she couldn't tell Calamity the truth about her dad. Perhaps if Calamity had known how much she was loved, she wouldn't have been placed in the predicament she was in now.

Calamity took the photo from Ruby's hands and placed it in her school bag. Her dad may not have loved her, but she still loved him. She didn't really remember him. She had only been two when he left and her mother didn't talk about him often. Every now and then, something would happen, or be said, that would remind her mother of him. Then she would divulge some information about him that Calamity soaked up like a sponge soaks up water.

These were the things that Calamity held onto, and helped her to feel as though she knew her dad and loved him. As she gathered the last of her things, she asked her friends about their family. Lucas nodded to Ruby to tell the story, and perched himself on the edge of Calamity's bed to listen.

"Our parents were teenagers themselves when they met and fell in love. We were conceived in their last year of school, and they were under the belief there was no-one better than them to raise us."

"So you are twins then?"

"Yep, twins. Anyway, we have spent the past sixteen years travelling around Australia, being home-schooled by our parents. We have had an amazing life. Seen a lot of beautiful places, and met a lot of unhappy kids. The best part about our life is our parents are so in tune with young people. They are so good at helping young people heal their relationship with their parents. Our parents look forward to us bringing them new kids to meet. Those children then become part of our extended family. We have got brothers and sisters up and down the coast and always have a place to stay when we visit their towns."

"Why do they want other people's children?"

"They don't want to keep them, Calamity. They just want them to have a grownup they can turn to, when they are troubled. Somebody reliable who will listen to their problems, and not push them aside or make them feel unimportant.

"Our parents are wonderful people, about the same age as your mother, but without the monetary worries that seem to plague and age other adults. Because of this, our parents are still quite childlike, and are always looking for new children to play with."

"Don't you ever get upset by other children taking your parents' love away from you?"

"Love doesn't work that way, Calamity. The more you love, the more it grows. You can never run short of love. You just make more."

"I don't understand."

"I know, but Mum and Dad will be able to help you comprehend this concept. They are very clever. That is why the government allows us to be home-schooled by them. Do you want to come and meet them?"

"Would they like me?"

"Oh, Calamity, they are going to love you."

Loretta found what she was looking for, and headed back to her daughter's room. This was going to be the last time her daughter locked her out, and she felt it was time they had a heart-to-heart chat about things. She loved her daughter. In fact she probably loved her too much.

She was so scared of losing Calamity, she was probably the one that was driving a wedge between them both, and chasing her daughter away. Loretta walked up the stairs, through the kitchen, into the lounge room, and down the hallway. Arriving at Calamity's door, she began loosening the screws that held the lock in place.

As she undid the last one, she opened the door and witnessed her daughter jumping through the open window, and running along the veranda. Loretta hurried to the window to see where Calamity was going. She spotted her running down the stairs with a girl and a boy leading the way.

"Calamity, no. Please come back," she screamed, but her daughter kept running. Loretta climbed out of the window and followed in their footsteps. She reached the edge of the driveway before she lost sight of them, after they crested the hill.

Thirteen

Once they had breached the hill, the teenagers turned left and ran towards the edge of the forest. After half an hour or so, they entered the forest and slid down the back of the hill to the bottom.

Ahead was an old, run-down barn that had two of its side walls missing. They ran to it, and climbed up on to the beam where they could see the abandoned farm. The grass was waist high in the paddocks, and there was a variety of weeds in flower, scattered throughout.

"What are we doing here? I thought we were going to see your parents?" Calamity asked.

"They are out seeing to some children in the neighbouring town. We've got an hour or so before they return. We thought you might like to chill out here for a while. No-one ever comes here," Ruby said.

"We heard you don't like Jacinta. How come?" Lucas asked.

Calamity's body stiffened at the mention of her name. Her eyes flashed with anger and her hands bunched into fists. "I don't want to talk about her."

"I do," Lucas replied. "Come on, Cal. Tell us why you don't like her."

"She's stupid."

"No, she's not. She's a straight A student. Choose your words better," Ruby encouraged.

"She dresses like a city brat."

Ruby said, "So do Hannah and Breanna. They wear the latest trend in clothes, and you still like them. Try again."

"She gets to do what she wants."

"So do you. You sneak out every day when your mamma is not home, and do whatever you want," Lucas responded. "Stop spitting out the fluffy stuff and go deeper. Why don't you like Jacinta? Uh, uh. Don't answer now. Think about it first."

Calamity brought up the image of Jacinta in her mind. She pictured her at the dining room table with her parents, playing one of their many board games. They always put Jacinta at the head of the table so she could reach better, and they could help her more easily. That was the first thing she hated about Jacinta. They put her first. Calamity's mum always put her second. In her mind, Calamity saw Jacinta as she had looked down at the river that morning.

Her blonde hair had been put up into two cute little buns, not like Princess Leia in the movies. Jacinta's buns were more to the back of her head. It was a hairstyle that had obviously been done by her mother.

That was number two. Calamity's mum spent mountains of time on her own looks, but couldn't take the time to put Calamity's hair up, like Jacinta's mum did, on a daily basis. Jacinta's buns looked cute. So too did the double or single braids her mother often did for her.

Jacinta always had the latest fashions. That morning at the river, she had been dressed in dark pink tights with matching high-tops. A light pink skirt sat over that, and she wore a white and dark pink striped, long-sleeved shirt on top. With her little blonde buns she was very cute, and Calamity was sure the boys would think so too.

She didn't stop to think that it would be a few years before the boys started noticing things like that. Calamity was lucky to get a pair of jeans and a new shirt for Christmas and her birthday. Not much more to hate than that.

Jacinta's parents worked somewhere in real-estate. Calamity was sure they got to see the new houses being built, and when they were completed, it was their task to find the buyers. When a house was finished, they often took Jacinta to have a look, before anyone else got to see. Calamity lived in an old, one story farm house. The new homes being built were two stories high, and were situated in estates divided into five acre blocks.

The occupants of these new estates were not expected to farm their land, but had enough space to have a few animals. A cow or a few goats, some chickens and ducks or a couple of pigs for a pet, along with the normal cats and dogs.

Jacinta could wander from room to room and pretend the house was hers. She could pretend to pick out her new room, and imagine herself living in the freshly painted bedroom. Oh wait, her house had been fully renovated before they moved in six months ago, and her bedroom was freshly painted. The reasons just kept piling up.

Jacinta was good at school stuff. She always seemed to know the correct answers, and all the teachers loved her. They would join in Jacinta's hand ball games at lunch, and she would be given the jobs of running around the school, collecting students for the Principal, when asked. She sometimes spent more time out of the classroom than she did inside, and it never seemed to affect her grades in any way. She was also good at sport.

It wasn't right that somebody was good at the smart stuff, and sport as well. *And* she was beautiful. People should just be good at one or the other, which would be the fair thing in life. Calamity felt she was average in looks, grades and sport, but knew she was gifted in language.

There had been a couple of kids who had come from Japan, and stayed a couple of years, before returning to their country. She had found that she was able to pick up their language quite easily. Pity that wasn't a part of the curriculum at her school. She might have received an A for once on her report card, and made her mother proud.

JEALOUSY MONSTERS

Jacinta's mum was always telling her daughter how proud she was of her. Calamity heard them every day when she sat outside their window, and listened to them talking to one another. Calamity never thought about how creepy her behaviour was. She was totally consumed with Jacinta and her life. If there had been a fairy godmother, Calamity would have stolen it way before now, and become the girl she so wanted to be.

"I don't hate Jacinta. I want to be her!" she said in astonishment.

"That's right, Calamity, you want to be Jacinta. If you stay with us, you will be," Lucas told her.

"What do you mean?"

"We will be your parents when ours are helping other children in need. We will play with you and put you first. We will bring you new clothes that make you feel beautiful and loved. Cal, you will never have to feel lonely, upset or angry ever again. We can help you make Jacinta wish she was you. Her parents still have to leave her to go to work. We don't have to work. We have everything we need at home. Our family is self-sufficient and wants for nothing. You can be a part of that, and Jacinta will be so jealous."

Ruby had taken out the camera that was hidden in her pocket and snuck a photo of Calamity. She had noticed Lucas shimmering, and realised that they were starting to lose negative energy from Calamity, by making her feel all those horrible sweet feelings. It was time to show the other children a picture of the new addition to their family. The increase in negative emotion, emanating from their six prisoners, should be enough to make their materialization stabilised enough to complete the capturing of this new one.

"We've got a surprise in store for you, sister. I just need an hour or so to make it perfect for you. Are you right to hang here with Lucas until my return? You will be safe in his company, and when I come for you, a gift will be waiting for your collection."

JEALOUSY MONSTERS

"Can't Lucas do that and you stay with me?"

"If there is no trust, there is no joining the family, Calamity."

"Of course I trust him," she said, not meaning it at all.

Ruby's smile was full of cunning and malice, and for once, Calamity wondered if she had made a mistake in coming with the pair of teenagers she hardly knew. "Look after my brother, Calamity. Make him happy, and the gift I have in store for you will be yours to keep forever."

Calamity looked at Lucas and wondered what she had to do to make him happy. She hoped it wasn't anything her mother would not approve of. She wasn't ready for any of that grown up stuff, and Lucas was a bit older than her, and probably liked that. "You are not going to hurt me, are you, Lucas?" she queried.

"Of course not," he said draping his arm over her shoulder. "Come on, let's have some fun," he said getting to his feet and climbing down the ladder. Calamity followed him, wondering where they were going. He led her towards a little shack further down the way. She worried that he was going to take her inside and close the door, but they simply skirted the outside, and wandered towards a stream that cut through the property. He bent down at the water's edge to see what was in there.

"Don't tell me you like to look for tadpoles and turtles too," she whined.

"Who likes to do that?"

"Jacinta."

"Hmmm, I should have guessed that, shouldn't I? No, I am looking for a particular type of rock."

"What does it look like?" she asked, bending down to peer at the water's edge herself.

"It doesn't matter what the colour is, but it must be flattish and smooth."

"What do you want it for?"

"To skip it across the water."

"To what?"

"Here, I'll show you," he said, holding up a suitable pebble. He placed the rock between his fingers and pulled his arm back. Then he flung it forward at speed and let the rock go. It bounced once, twice, three times across the top of the water, before sinking in the middle of the stream.

Lucas searched for another one and gave it to Calamity. "Try it." She copied what she thought he had done, and the rock sank without bouncing. "That's okay. You just let your arm fall instead of keeping it flat. Here's another one, try again."

She pulled her arm back, and made sure she kept it parallel to the ground. She brought it forward at great speed, as though she was hitting a tennis ball, and flung the little pebble out over the water. It skipped once, then twice before sinking into the water. She giggled with delight while Lucas told her how spectacular that had been. Calamity searched for another pebble and found two. She gave one to Lucas and kept one for herself.

They flung their pebbles together in competition to see who could make their pebble go further. Calamity was surprised to see hers skip just ahead of his before disappearing into the depths. "Beginners luck," he told her.

She began looking for another, when he motioned for her to follow him. This was turning out to be not so bad after all, and she wondered what they were going to do next. He took her further away from the barn, and closer to the windmill.

"Are you afraid of heights?"

"I climb trees, don't I?"

"Righty-o, up you go."

Fourteen

They climbed until they were situated just below the blades. There they perched on the horizontal support, and looked out over the countryside. There were many farms lying between them and the mountains.

The mist that usually surrounded the mountains had disappeared with the warmth of the day. They stood majestically above everything else, and she pondered why her mother had never taken her up there, and what lay beyond.

"Have you ever been there, to the mountains, I mean?" Calamity asked Lucas.

"Yeah. The view from up there is even better than this. There are creatures that live there amongst the trees and the forest floor that I have never seen anywhere else."

"Like what?"

"You know, birds and mammals and stuff. It is probably because up there, it is easy to stay still for a long period of time. The creatures kind of become used to you being there, so they come out of hiding. I am sure they probably live elsewhere, too, they are just easier to spot in there."

"Can we go there sometime?" Calamity asked.

"Sure. We would need to leave at first light so we could make the most of it. It takes a couple of hours to get there by car, so I'll ask my parents when I introduce you to them."

"Maybe we should wait a bit before throwing something like that at them. They might not want me hanging around, if they feel I am going to create work for them."

"Don't be silly, Cal. They would feel privileged to share your first time in seeing a place as beautiful as the mountains. It would be like them seeing it for the first time all over again."

"Well, if you are sure." She looked out over the landscape and saw a couple of adults ploughing the field, way off in the distance. She wondered where their kids were, and thought perhaps they were a young couple who hadn't had any yet. She imagined a bunch of brothers out there in the field helping their dad complete his work, and realised how much she wished she had siblings.

At least that was something she couldn't be jealous of Jacinta for. Jacinta was an only child as well. "I've always wanted an older brother," she said aloud. "I'm glad I ran into you and Ruby the other day during the storm. Imagine if it had been sunny. We might have missed each other."

"Yeah, imagine that," Lucas said.

"What's that over there? It looks like a door has been placed on the side of the hill," Calamity said with curiosity in her voice.

"Let's go check it out."

They climbed down the windmill carefully. It had been a lot easier climbing up than it seemed going down. The steel appeared a lot more slippery beneath her feet and her hands became sweaty from fear. "I don't know if I can get down again," Calamity said with a high-pitched voice that scared her more than she already felt.

"You'll be okay. Just like climbing out of a tree. Don't think about what you are doing and go by instinct. Your instincts are good, Cal. Trust in them and you'll be okay."

His little pep talk worked and before she knew it, she was low enough to leap off and touch solid ground. Lucas allowed Calamity to lead the way this time. 'Humans are so predictable,' he thought. He contemplated the thought that there might be more creatures out there like him and Ruby, and wondered how he might go about finding out if that was true. That was something he would take up with Ruby, when they had a moment alone together.

Calamity half skipped, half jogged to the place she had seen from her vantage point on the windmill. True enough, there on the side of the hill was a set of white doors, with mud streaked windows that were too dirty to see through. She tested the handle and found it to be unresisting beneath her grip. "Pht," said the doors, as the suction holding them together was released. Then the doors clunked as they separated a few centimetres from each other, and a smell of damp earth assaulted their senses.

"I don't think we should go in there. Let's go back to the barn and wait for Ruby. I am sure she will be back soon, and will be worried if we aren't there when she returns."

"Where's your sense of adventure? This is what big brothers are for. To make their little sisters feel protected, and show them things they are too frightened to see on their own. What could be so dangerous in there?"

"What wouldn't be?"

"Oh, Calamity, you are such a girly-girl. Ruby would come in there with me." When Calamity hesitated he pushed her a little further. "So would Jacinta."

That did it. She pushed the doors open, and stormed inside without any heed for danger. She took two steps and then her feet went out from under her. Down, down, down she slid on her bottom, screaming with terror. Thump. She suddenly stopped, with her legs tucked painfully beneath her. This time, however, Force wasn't there to make her feel better.

Calamity stood up and rubbed her backside and legs, willing the pain to go away. It didn't hurt that much and she could tell the pain wouldn't last for too long. She had ended up in a large cave like structure.

The roof was at least five metres above her head with jagged bits of rock pointing downwards. The sides were made of rock, and it was cold and dark. The air smelled musty making the insides of her nose hurt a little. There was a golden light emanating from further inside the cave, and she realised that was how she was able to see anything at all.

Calamity looked back the way she had come to see a flicker of movement. She realised too late, that Lucas was on his way down. He bowled her over, landing smack, bang on top of her. Great, now the breath had been knocked out of her, and her front was hurting as much as her back.

He peered into her face and asked, "Why didn't you move out of the way?"

"I didn't even think about your entry into the cavern. I was too surprised by the surroundings," Calamity gasped.

He kissed her on the tip of her nose causing her to blush, and stood up, helping her to her feet. Lucas took a few minutes to get his bearings and poked around. "I think our only option is to head towards the light."

Calamity moved back to the slide that had been their entry, but noticed it was way too steep and slippery to be able to return the way they had entered. With the glow of light being the only exit from the room they had found themselves in, she had to agree with him. He led her toward the light and through a lower, hollowed out gap in the rock which opened up into another cavernous room. Flamed torches rested in wall brackets mounted at three metre intervals, casting a soft glow over everything in the room.

A pool of water, with raised sides and steam swirling from the top, was situated in the middle of the room. The air quality had changed. It was more humid than the room before. Calamity walked to the water and held out a finger to plunge beneath the surface. Lucas yelled at her to stop, and picked up a stick lying on the ground.

He dipped the end of the stick into the water and pulled it out again. The end of the stick had not disappeared, confirming his suspicion that the water was not highly acidic. He felt the end of the stick and found the wetness to be very warm. So the water temperature was high, and Calamity would most likely have burnt herself had she placed her finger in there. He allowed her to touch the stick and she thanked him for his warning shout.

They looked around, and Calamity found she could take the burning torch off the wall. It was heavier than expected and she handed it to Lucas who was stronger than her. He lifted it above his head, looking for a way out of the room other than the one they had entered through.

"Look at the drawings on the walls. I wonder who did them," Calamity said.

"I don't know," Lucas replied.

There was nothing but solid rock above their heads. Next he shone the torch down low, following the walls until he found a small tunnel they could squeeze through.

"Do you want to go first or would you prefer me to?" he asked, pointing at the tunnel.

"You go and I will follow."

He pushed the torch through in front of him, before lying on the ground.

"Take hold of my ankle so you won't be frightened once the light disappears," he suggested.

She, too, lay on the ground and, grabbing his ankle, they commando crawled their way through the long, dark, coffin-like tunnel. Calamity's heart was in her throat and she thought she would literally choke on her fear. If Lucas had not been there, she was sure she would have died of fright, right there in that moment.

As her head breached the exit, she took her first breath of freedom, much like a new baby after having been born. She found herself in a well-lit room completely constructed of concrete. She got to her feet and looked around the room. Six other children gazed at her with such loathing that she wished she was invisible.

Calamity wanted to say something but couldn't find any words that would be appropriate. She had never felt so unwelcome in her life and wondered what she had done to deserve their hatred. Lucas moved to the left and all twelve eyes followed him. In that moment, Calamity realised they were unhappy with Lucas, not her. One of the boys left the group to stand in front of her. "Welcome to hell," he said.

Fifteen

Loretta ran back home to call the police, then realised they would be at the bake sale. She jumped in the car instead, and hooned down the road to the church.

The ladies on the afternoon shift were selling to their first customers of the day, when Loretta 'drifted' her car around the corner and screeched to a halt in the carpark. The women stood with their mouths wide open. The men clapped and yahooed in appreciation of her driving prowess.

Loretta threw the door open before yanking on the handbrake. She screamed that her daughter had just jumped out of her bedroom window, and taken off with two strangers. People left the stalls to rush to her side, so they could hear the whole story first hand. It gave them more credibility when they spread the story, if they could say they heard it from the horse's mouth.

Force had just placed half a lamington, a small square of sponge cake smothered in chocolate icing and coconut, into his mouth when the commotion started. He hurried over to her, chewing as quickly as he could. Swallowing half the cake before it was in a manageable state, he nearly choked on the coconut. He ended up with a burning sensation all the way down his throat and felt pain developing in his chest area. 'Great, now I'm going to have to deal with indigestion as well,' he thought.

"Okay, everybody, give the lady some space and go back to your stalls."

"Who are you to tell us what to do?" asked one of the stall holders.

"Liam Force from Starlight Investigations," he stated holding up his credentials. "I am here on official business looking into the disappearances of the local children. I can assure you all, that this episode is not something to be worried about."

"How can you say that? You don't even know what has happened."

Force turned to Loretta but before he could ask his question, she got her own in. "What do you think you are doing pretending to be an investigator?"

"I'm sorry?"

"Dr. Force, remember?" she said angrily, shoving the business card she had been given earlier, under his nose.

"That is my twin brother," he replied, getting the investigator business card out of his wallet and handing it to her. He waited until he saw she had registered the new information, before saying, "Now, Miss . . ." He was interrupted by Loretta who introduced herself.

"My name is Loretta."

"Okay, Loretta, did you and your daughter have a disagreement just prior to her jumping out the window?"

"Well, yes."

"And does your daughter have a habit of running away from the issues that are troubling her?"

"Yes, she does, but . . ."

"See, folks, there has been no kidnapping here. Go back to your business. I will help this lovely young woman find her runaway daughter, and see if I can get her to return home."

The people at the bake sale were disappointed to not have a fully blown disaster on their hands. Their life was simple, but boring, unlike their city cousins. Every now and then, they hoped for something exciting to happen in their lives. Rather than create the excitement themselves, they waited for some tragedy to occur to give them something new to talk about.

Of course, none of them wished total devastation to occur to their friends or themselves. They all wanted a happy ending, after all. But something that created a generous amount of interest certainly wouldn't go astray. Like that nasty business about the missing children. If one of their own had disappeared, well that would definitely have been something worth getting together for, to commiserate properly, of course.

"He's really your brother?" Loretta asked Force.

"Yeah, he really is. Were you injured?"

"No, my daughter. It's a long story that we don't have time for now."

"Any idea where to start looking?"

"No. I don't even know her anymore," she said disheartened.

"Come on, let's go back to your place, and I'll see if I can track her footsteps."

JEALOUSY MONSTERS

They walked to her car with what felt like a million eyes watching them. She was young and on her own with a twelve year old girl. She was very pretty, and still took good care of herself and her weight. He was young and handsome, with muscles that showed he hit the gym regularly.

Tongues had started wagging before he had even slid into the passenger seat. By the time they had arrived back at her place, they were already in a full-blown relationship with talk of wedding bells in the near future.

Loretta knew how her busybody neighbours would react, and couldn't even care less. She knew what their conversations would be about, as they gossiped with their customers. It certainly wouldn't be about her missing daughter.

No, their talk would be all about how she was hooking up with the young man who was drifting through. 'Let them talk about me,' she thought. While they were talking about her, they were leaving her baby alone, and that suited her just fine.

Maybe she should listen to the conversation her mind was going on about, in an attempt to guess what they might be saying. He looked exactly the same as his brother, and maybe this one *wasn't* married. This one seemed as helpful and decent as the other. It wouldn't hurt to try again, once her daughter had been found safe and sound.

Calamity deserved a decent male in her life. Someone she could depend on who would make her feel loved and protected, as a daughter should be. No-one around here fitted that bill.

She pulled up beside her front stairs, and led him to the veranda outside her daughter's room. It would be nice to have something warm inside his belly before he followed Calamity's trail. He asked Loretta if she wouldn't mind making him a cup of coffee while he had a look around outside.

Force noticed the chipped paint and indents in the wood of Calamity's bedroom windows. He wondered if it was Calamity, Ruby or Lucas who had put them there. As Loretta went inside to put the kettle on, she thought about changing into something more suitable for trudging all over the countryside. Force picked up on her thoughts and burst her bubble.

"Loretta, you know you aren't coming with me, right?" he called, from the veranda.

"No way! She is my baby and I am *definitely* coming with you," she said, marching outside to challenge him.

"I need you to stay here in case she comes home. You have my card with my mobile number on it and can ring me anytime to get an update."

"But she won't even know who you are. She won't trust you."

"She has met my twin, so she won't be frightened when she sees me. Besides, you would be surprised at my ability to get children to trust me. It is why they have put me in this position in the first place. If I tell a kid to drop to the floor, they don't even question my motives, they just do it. It has saved many a child's life."

"Please, don't make me stay here on my own, wondering what is going on."

"I'm sorry, Loretta. It is the only way I can get her back to you safely, if she has decided she is not coming home. Things will be okay, you'll see. Now if I could please have that cup of coffee, I will be on my way, and get home more quickly with your daughter."

Loretta walked inside with tears in her eyes. There was nothing worse for her, than being made to hang around, and wait for some sort of news. The last time she had been made to do that, was when her husband had been shot, and he was in surgery fighting for his life.

They had worked on him for six hours, only to tell her after, that they had been unsuccessful in their endeavours to remove the bullet. He would probably not live through the night. He had died a couple of hours after that. Now, here was a dreamboat, giving her hope that she would see her daughter again. Then telling her she would have to wait until he returned in some unspecified amount of time. No, she wasn't going to cop that.

While she waited for the kettle to boil, she went to the hallway cupboard and pulled a small box from the top drawer. Inside was the mobile phone that she had planned to give to Calamity next Friday for her birthday.

She took the sim card from her purse, and replaced it in the phone. She had removed it previously in case Calamity found the phone hidden in the drawer. Ringing the number given to her to activate the phone, she requested the GPS locator function be turned on, and linked to her own mobile phone. The kettle boiled and she made his cup of coffee. When she brought the cup outside, she found him up near the fence line, looking in the dirt.

"Coffee," she called to him. He looked up and smiled. Oh, he was so lovely to look at. He made his way back to the house, and sat on the veranda while he drank his cup of coffee and ate the biscuits she had placed on a plate for him. "I was wondering if you could give this to Calamity when you see her. I was going to give it to her Friday, but perhaps it will help you in your endeavours to get her to come home."

"You make it sound like she has really run away."

"She had a backpack with her, full of clothes and her favourite bear. I think she is planning on being gone for a while," she said as a tear rolled down her cheek.

He leaned forward and wiped it away. "She has no intentions of leaving you, Loretta," he told her.

"What makes you think she wants to come home?"

"The kids that she left with, was one a boy and one a girl?"

"Yeah. They were a lot older than Calamity. I don't know where she would know them from. I haven't seen them at school."

"Are you at the school often?"

"Yeah, I help out at the canteen."

"And you have never seen them before?"

"No, never. They were in Calamity's bedroom, Liam! They must have climbed through the window. How could my daughter let somebody influence her like that?"

"Loretta, these kids are professionals at what they do, but so am I. Please try not to worry about her. Our trip here has been very educational, and my brother and I are aware of what we are dealing with now. You will be reunited with your daughter very shortly."

"You lied back there, didn't you? She's in danger, isn't she?"

"Yes, I lied back there. It would be an absolute nightmare having all of those vigilantes out there messing up the tracks, and maybe chasing those two troublemakers underground again. Calamity is not in any danger. They need her alive and healthy and will do everything in their power to ensure she stays that way."

"How do you know?"

"I can't tell you, Loretta, you just have to trust me."

He stood to leave, but she had other ideas.

Sixteen

Loretta wrapped her arms around his waist and hugged him tightly. "Thank you for helping me. Please give Calamity the phone as soon as you can."

He looked into her eyes, and promised he would do what he could to get her daughter home safe and sound. She stood on her tiptoes and planted a kiss on his lips.

JEALOUSY MONSTERS

He was taken by surprise and froze for a second, before his lips moved of their own volition. Soon he was kissing her back. Scout, who had caught up to Force when he was standing at the fence line and entered his pocket, poked her head out to see why it had gone quiet, and was horrified to see them smooching. She ducked back into his pocket and punched him as hard as she could. He grunted and broke off the kiss.

"I'll see you as soon as I can," he told her breathlessly, moving towards the stairs outside Calamity's room.

"Ring me every hour to let me know you are okay, and haven't been caught yourself. If I don't hear from you, I will phone the police."

"No, don't do that. You might make them disappear. Ring my brother, he will know who to contact."

He made his way down the stairs, and retraced his steps to the location where he had been, when she had called him for coffee. He leaned down once more and looked at the ground, picking up Calamity's trail. He saw the slight change in the way the grass was lying, and picked out the path he was to take to follow them.

Force took off for the hills while Scout stood seething in his pocket. As soon as she felt she was far enough away to not be seen by the mother, Scout launched herself from his pocket and landed on his shoulder. From there, she was able to yell and scream at him as much as she wanted and knew she would be heard.

"Scout, tell me what you really think!" he said.

"I just did. Weren't you listening?"

"Yes. Let me rephrase. Tell me what you really want to know?"

"Why were you kissing her? Did you like it?"

"I kissed her because she took me by surprise and kissed me, and yes, I liked it."

"Are you going to do it again?"

"I don't know, would it matter if I did?"

"Of course not," Scout said, but knew she was lying. She didn't want Force kissing other women, she wanted him to kiss her. Scout knew that was impossible, she was a fairy and he was a Gatherer. But that didn't change the feelings she had developed for him, and they couldn't seem to be undeveloped.

"Why did you punch me?"

"They have got Calamity. You don't have time to stand around kissing every woman you meet."

"I don't kiss . . . Are you jealous, Scout?" Force said coming to a realisation.

"Don't be ridiculous."

"You want to kiss me?"

Scout didn't say a word. She flew back into his pocket and sulked in silence. Force was shaken by this sudden revelation. He loved Scout, very much, but wasn't sure if he loved her like that.

He had never really thought about kissing her, except for a few hours ago, and remembered he wasn't averse to the idea then. Scout was his colleague. Someone he relied on to find the creatures, so that he could catch them and hand them over to the Collectors.

What would happen if they had a relationship with one another? Would it become complicated and unworkable? Would they be reprimanded by their superiors and reassigned to other Locators and Gatherers? Maybe it wouldn't be a good idea to see where it might lead, since the last few thoughts were all negative and fearful. He realised he loved her too much, to risk losing her because of a kiss.

Force had lost the trail when his thoughts had gone off on a tangent, so he stood still and viewed his surroundings. He soon picked up Calamity's trail and continued on, finding himself in front of an old run down barn.

Surveying his surrounds, he soon discovered two tracks leading in one direction, and one track leading in another. He was pretty sure the two tracks belonged to Lucas and Calamity. The right one was heavier than the others, and the footprint of the one on the left was shorter than the one leaving the other way.

JEALOUSY MONSTERS

Force was confused. Why would the creatures split up? Calamity obviously felt safe enough with Lucas, as there was no evidence of a struggle. Calamity seemed to have followed him of her own free will.

He had to admit, these creatures were good at catching their prey. Scout and he had to be better, and he was no longer sure they were up to the task. There seemed to be some underlying feelings between them both that he hadn't been aware of. He was pretty sure she was brooding in his pocket. He was used to using his powers to catch and hold the creatures. For this case, that would become Scout's task. His obligation extended to diffusing the children's negative emotions, hence releasing the creatures from their Earthly existence. *'That's it!'* he thought.

"Scout!"

"What?" she shouted at him from his pocket.

"Scout, come out here right now!"

"NO!"

Force waited to see if she would come out, and when she didn't, he gave her one more chance. "If you don't come out right now, I am going to put my hand in my pocket and I am not sure where I will be grabbing."

Scout flew out of his pocket so fast she nearly missed her mark. She flew up into his face and pointed her finger at him, hurling abuse.

"I don't know what has gotten into you to use that sort of language, but we'll talk about that later. Will you stop yelling at me and stabbing your finger in the air. Don't you know that kills fairies?"

She stopped immediately and looked at him with a horrified expression on her face. She placed her face in her hands and wept uncontrollably. Force gently tickled the back of her hands and asked her to look at him. She raised her tear-streaked face but refused to raise her eyes.

"Oh, Scout, you didn't kill any fairies by stabbing your finger in the air. I'm sorry I said that. You know fairies can only be permanently killed when children stop believing in them. As long as children believe in magic, there will always be magical creatures to delight them," he reminded her.

She flew to his upheld finger and hugged it, kissing the tip. His finger tingled where her lips had touched his skin, which was not unpleasant at all. "I know how to defeat the monsters. We can't hand them over to the Collectors, because they aren't the type of creatures that can be housed in Mystique. Neither can we kill them. The only way to defeat the monsters is to help the children lose their feelings of jealousy, and the creatures should simply disappear."

Scout was amazed she had not thought of that earlier. Once again, Force was the one who would save the day, and she would sit in the background in case there was a further need for her services. He knew now which set of tracks they needed to follow.

The children were the key to stopping the creatures, which made perfect sense, since the creatures were created by the children in the first place. Down the hill he walked, with Scout perched on his shoulder once more. He didn't bother much with the scenery, mostly keeping his head down to make sure he didn't lose his way again.

He found the windmill which was covered in the creature's mist. It seemed like Lucas and Calamity had spent a bit of time hanging out in this part of the clearing. He wondered why, but not enough to climb the structure himself. He thought about transforming into a creature, to see what the children would have seen when they climbed the structure, but was afraid of losing the mobile phone Loretta had given him.

"Scout, will you fly to the top of the mist and tell me what you see?"

"Okay. There is a clear view of the mountain ranges from up on top of the windmill stand. From what I have seen of Calamity, I think this is what would have captured her attention." Scout landed back on Force's shoulder and they continued on their journey, until the trail ended at the side of a hill. There was no indication of where the pair had gone next. The footsteps and crumpled grass simply ended in front of him.

Force tried to pick up on Calamity's thoughts but could not feel her anywhere. Was she dead? No, that didn't make sense. The creatures needed her alive to keep them solid. There were no scuff marks on the hillside, where the pair may have climbed their way up. Neither could he find any hidden trapdoors on the ground where they may have disappeared below.

He asked Scout for her thoughts, but she was just as stumped as he was. She flew to the hill to take a closer look, and suddenly disappeared from view. One second he saw her, the next she was gone. He held out his hand and ran it over the spot where she disappeared. His finger hooked up on something hard, and opened the door that had been invisible to them both, presenting a hole where there had been grass moments before.

"Scout," he called.

"I'm okay. It's like a cave in here. Don't come in. I kind of got sucked in through the door itself and it was the most repulsive feeling I've ever had. I'll go check out the support structure, and let you know if it is safe or not for you to come in."

"Wait. Scout." She didn't answer him. He called again without a reply. Force decided to meld with her mind and take the journey with her. He could no longer sense her. There must be some type of mystical barrier blocking his control over Spirit. He chose to take her advice and sat in wait for her to return with news.

Seventeen

Jacinta was entering the church grounds, when she saw the car screaming down the road. She watched with interest as it slewed around the corner and slid into the car park. She became even more interested, when she saw a pretty woman in a fancy dress, jump out and begin yelling at everyone.

Jacinta sprinted to the tables to hear what was going on. That was Calamity's mum, and she sure was upset about something. Some man had gone over to Mrs. Landscombe and asked the onlookers to go back to their stalls.

Jacinta attempted to move closer to the action, when Mrs. Cassidy grabbed hold of her arm and told her that what was going on was none of her business. She led her to the edge of the church grounds, and encouraged her to go play with the other kids.

"Hello, Jacinta," Justine said casually, while Mrs. Cassidy watched with her eagle eyes.

"Hello, everyone," Jacinta replied with a smile.

Mrs. Cassidy nodded her head in approval and moved away to catch up on what she had missed.

"Did you hear what was going on over there?" Donovan asked Jacinta.

"I think Calamity had a fight with her mum again. Her mum thinks she has been kidnapped."

"Are you serious? That's ridiculous. No wonder Calamity doesn't want us hanging around you," Breanna stated.

"No, I'm telling the truth. That man over there told everyone there hasn't been a kidnapping, so maybe there really has. Have you ever seen Calamity's mum react that way before?"

"No," William said. "Her mum is usually pretty normal."

"Something is going on," Jacinta told them. "There are a couple of teenagers hanging around up in the hills. They might have something to do with Calamity running off on her mum."

"So a couple of kids are up in the hills. Whoop-dee-doo, Jacinta. You spend a lot of time up there, too," Hannah said.

"Yeah, but these kids are different. There is something off about them. They really creep me out."

"Yeah, well, you really creep me out," Hannah huffed.

"Calamity could be in real trouble, and you just want to stand there giving me a hard time," Jacinta said angrily. "Fine, I'll find out what is going on by myself."

Jacinta turned and began walking back to the hills. Once she had put a couple of hundred metres between herself and the kids left behind, she called to Scout and blew a kiss, just like she had been told. Scout appeared before her, fluttering in the air at eye level.

"Scout, you came!"

"Of course I did. You called me."

"Is Calamity in trouble?"

"Yeah, I think so. Her mum saw Calamity jump out of the bedroom window, and run off with two teenagers she doesn't know. Do you know who they are, Jacinta?"

"Maybe. There have been a couple of older kids hanging around the place."

"Do you know where they live?"

"No, I don't," she replied.

JEALOUSY MONSTERS

"Jacinta, I have to go. Stay in town with everybody else until your parents get home, okay?"

"Yeah, sure," she lied.

Scout looked back at the church grounds and saw Force leaving with Loretta. She knew where they were going, so she wasn't worried about losing him. Although her wings were fast, they weren't as fast as the car, so it took her a bit longer to get there. By the time she had arrived, Force was standing at the fence line looking for the trio's trail. She carefully made her way to his pocket without being seen, and ducked inside.

Jacinta decided to go home first, and grab some more supplies. She would need some more bottled water, as she only had the one bottle, and there was nowhere to refill it other than the stream. She wasn't willing to risk picking up a water-borne germ that might make her sick.

Some more food wouldn't go astray either. She wouldn't be back until dinner time and would need something to stop her tummy from grumbling. The last thing she wanted was for her position to be given away by a grumbly tummy, if she was hiding from the baddies. Jacinta had seen the movies and she knew how to be prepared.

She reached the bottom of her street before she heard somebody following behind her. Jacinta spun around on her heels to find Calamity's friends, frozen in their tracks, trying not to bring attention to themselves. She burst out laughing, bringing a smile to the children's faces.

"What do you think you are doing?" she asked them all.

"We thought we could help you look for Calamity," William said.

"That is what you are doing, isn't it?" questioned Hannah.

"Yeah. I just thought I should pick up some supplies first," Jacinta said.

"So, can we come?" Breanna asked.

"Yes, you can come, but if you drop behind, you get left behind. This is not an army mission, you realise," Jacinta told them.

"You are so weird," Justine remarked.

They went to Jacinta's place with her, and grabbed some dried fruit, nuts and a popper each from the cupboard. Jacinta filled up another two water bottles from the hose outside. The children were not opposed to drinking from the stream and didn't want to carry their own water. She grabbed a couple of bananas for each child, and placed them in her backpack. William and Donovan already had hats, so she grabbed all of the hats she could find for the others. Prepared and ready, they headed for the hills where Jacinta had seen the teenagers last.

The children had to admit, Jacinta seemed to know what she was doing, and was acting like a pretty good leader. They were a bit confused by Calamity's aversion to her, even though some of them thought she was a bit strange.

Of course, that could simply be because they didn't know her very well. They were all in the same class and knew she was smart and all, but had never taken the time to get to know her likes and dislikes. Calamity saw to that.

They followed the rise and fall of the land. They walked together in harmony, sometimes singing and sometimes laughing at someone's joke. Jacinta told the kids she didn't mean to be rude, and they could tell her it was none of her business if they wanted, but she wondered why Donovan and William shaved their heads.

Donovan was the one who answered her question. "I was diagnosed with cancer a couple of months ago. Chemo made my hair fall out. William, being my identical twin, was worried I would look at him and become jealous, so he decided to shave his head to look like me."

"Is that true?" Jacinta asked, looking at William.

"Damn straight," William confirmed.

"What sort of cancer do you have?"

"Childhood Leukaemia. They hope I will grow out of it."

"How come William doesn't have it too?"

"They don't know. The doctors are using us as a case study. They think he might get it, too, but it is just taking a bit longer to develop in him."

"Wow, I'm sorry. There's the barn. We just need to go another hundred or so metres and then turn left into the woods. There is an old, run-down set of swings in there where the pair often hang out."

"How do you know all this?" Jeremy asked, speaking for the first time.

"I spend a lot of time up here. Calamity quite often chases me away from the river and the park. She doesn't come up here and I can spend my time in peace."

Justine said, "Jacinta, we are really sorry about the way we have been treating you. Calamity has been our friend forever and we have always done whatever she says. When we find Calamity, we are going to tell her we want to be your friends, and if she has a problem with that, she will just have to deal with it. Right, guys?"

"Right," they said in unison.

Jacinta's mood brightened considerably. She had always believed that if you wished for something long enough, eventually your wish would come true. Somehow this would all work out, and Calamity and she would become really good friends.

That is what Jacinta wanted and she wouldn't stop trying to make that happen. She just had to keep letting Calamity know that she wanted to be friends. They reached the barn, and the boys were ecstatic.

"Look at this place. This could be our new clubhouse," Donovan said.

"This is perfect," agreed William.

The girls looked at the ruins before them, and raised their eyebrows. Jeremy aligned himself with the girls.

"It's a wreck," he told the brothers. "There are only two walls still standing. It's not weatherproof or anything."

JEALOUSY MONSTERS

"No, but it's ours. Nobody comes here, or it would be in better shape. We could do, and be, whatever we want," William said excitedly.

"What about the teenagers. There is a number of hay bales pushed together over there, which could have been used as a make-shift bed. Maybe this is where they have been sleeping?" Jeremy suggested.

"Hmmm, maybe, but they would soon find somewhere else if it was suddenly taken over by eight twelve-year-olds," William chuckled. "Anyway, it's not like we are going to sleep here. Our parents would never allow that. No, this will just be our daytime clubhouse," Donovan stated.

Jacinta found their conversation fascinating. She was very hopeful that she would be able to become a regular part of their group. She led them from the barn to the swing, and found Lucas sitting in wait.

"Hello, there, friends of Calamity. Welcome to my forest."

"Where is Calamity?" Jacinta demanded.

"Well, as you can see, she is not here."

"Where is she then?" asked Breanna.

"I don't know. I haven't seen her for a while. I am surprised to see all of you though, especially with Jacinta. Calamity will not be pleased to learn of your treachery."

"What treachery? God, he is even weirder than Jacinta," Justine complained.

"Were you, or were you not, supposed to hang out with Jacinta?"

"Calamity didn't want us hanging out with Jacinta," Jeremy remarked, "but she doesn't really know her. Calamity would like Jacinta, if she gave herself the chance to get to know her."

"And therein lies the treachery. Calamity said don't play with her, and yet here you all are, together." Lucas got up off the swing and walked amongst the children. "What naughty, naughty friends you all are." He walked behind a tree and disappeared.

The kids freaked out a bit. Jacinta told them to stay where they were, while she entered the woods to look for Lucas. Returning a few minutes later, she admitted she couldn't find him. "Are we dealing with the supernatural here?" Hannah enquired.

"Don't be silly, Hannah. The Supernatural was created by writers and movie makers to scare people and make money. It's not real." Jeremy assured her.

"Actually, the Supernatural was created by the Catholic church to scare people into turning to God," Breanna said.

"Says the girl whose mum is in charge of the church committee," William laughed.

"So I should know what I am talking about then, shouldn't I!" she blasted.

"I believe in the Supernatural," Jacinta said quietly.

"Really," Hannah replied.

"Yeah, I even know a fairy."

The children burst into fits of laughter. They laughed until their sides hurt and just kept on laughing. They didn't stop, even when they saw

how serious Jacinta was. "I can prove it to you.
Scout," she called and blew her a kiss.

Eighteen

Scout appeared before her within seconds. "Oh, Jacinta, you couldn't have called me at a worse time." Scout noticed the other kids, and was disappointed by Jacinta's poor decision. "You promised you would keep our secret."

Force had warned her that kids couldn't be trusted. He had told her of many times when he had been required to use his special powers to erase the memories pertaining to him and his abilities. Children were simply incapable of keeping a secret as big as that.

"Whoa, how are you doing that?" Hannah asked Jacinta.

"Jacinta is not doing anything. My name is Scout, and I am a Fairy," she sighed.

The children crowded around her disbelievingly. Their eyes saw Scout fluttering in the air, but their minds told them fairies didn't exist, and that this must be some kind of trick. Scout flew above each of their heads and crumped a couple of times, sprinkling dust over their bodies.

"Have you seen Peter Pan? Yeah? Then think a happy thought." They did and levitated.

She was asked questions about where she came from, how old she was, how long she had been on Earth, were there more like her. They plied Jacinta with questions as well. Scout just wanted to get away. She had been close to finding Calamity and then Jacinta had called her away. Now Force was sitting outside the cave, unprotected and unaware of how close he was

204

to the creatures' lair, and finding the missing children. She had to get back to him.

"I don't suppose there is any use in asking you kids to keep my existence a secret? Jacinta couldn't, so I suppose you won't be able to either."

"It is easier to keep a secret when there is more than one person keeping it," Hannah told her. "When you have somebody to discuss the secret with, there is no great desire to unload the burden."

"Well, it would be really nice if you were able to keep me to yourselves. Jacinta, I was really close to finding the monsters that are stealing the children, and I think Calamity is with them. I have to get back to where I was, before you called. Please don't call me away again."

"I'm sorry, Scout, I just wanted to spend some time with you."

"No, you just wanted to show me off to your friends. I am not a possession, Jacinta."

"No, you are right. But we can help."

"It is too dangerous."

"There are two of them and seven of us, plus you," Jeremy said trying to convince her to let them help.

"I don't think so."

"They are only a couple of teenagers, aren't they?" Jeremy persisted.

"Not exactly. We, my partner and I, believe these particular monsters are not your everyday monsters. We are sure they were created from the emotions of jealous children."

"They are not real?" Jacinta asked.

"Not yet, but they are really close to being so. Imagine the power the creatures will receive if all of them walked in with you. Calamity's jealousy gauge would go through the roof."

"Then I will stay out of the way, but please don't make me stay behind. I am the one who has known where they were the whole time, and pieced it together."

"Actually, you being there is exactly what we need. With the monsters no longer in spirit form, their solid bodies would be way easier to confine until we can remove their life force, and make them disappear forever. We have to hurry. Do you know where the large windmill is, Jacinta? Past the windmill and up on the hill, you will find a man sitting in wait. He is my friend, Force. Tell him I sent you to help."

"Where are you going?"

"I need to find another way in. Tell Force not to enter the cavern. He is too big to fit through the tunnel. Ask him to make sure the children are not brought out through there and taken to a new hideout. Now go. Hurry, all of you."

The children found their way to Force. They didn't dillydally, nor did they waste time talking to one another. Force jumped to his feet in surprise, as he watched them run towards him. He racked his brain on what to do, and came up blank.

"Scout, we have company arriving in a few minutes. What's in there?" No answer. "Damn it, Scout."

He connected with her mind, and was surprised to discover she wasn't in the cavern. He quickly picked up on the threads of her interaction with the children, and saw that she was flying through the trees. He had flashes of the interior of the cavern, and knew he could increase the size of the tunnel with his earth powers, and not cause a cave-in. With Scout looking for another way in, he just had to wait until she discovered the entry, before making his move.

Nineteen

Jacinta stumbled over her words as she attempted to tell him the reason they were there. She stopped, took a deep breath and started again.

Force, who already knew everything thanks to his super powers, allowed her the opportunity to tell him what was going on. He knew how important it was for her to feel as though she was helping a fellow human being.

Force thanked her for passing on the information, and explained to the children how dangerous their actions had been. He told them he was an investigator, and unfortunately, in his line of work, he came across cases where children had made poor choices, and died as a result. He reminded them that the proper procedure for an incident like this was to call the police, as they had spent years training for serious issues like these to keep the public safe.

The children promised they would follow proper procedures next time. Force didn't believe them. They were full of adventurous spirit, and he realised that, unless they were extremely fortunate, it would take a tragedy to stop them from risk-taking behaviour.

The children asked him to ·explain his proposed plan of action. He told them he was waiting for Scout to find the other entry point, before the eight of them stormed the establishment. They chatted energetically to him about the part each of them was to play. While the children shared their food and water with Force, he discussed the order in which they would enter.

"Will the teenagers be there?" Jacinta asked.

"They go by the names of Lucas and Ruby, and I'm not sure. I can't read them at the moment, so they must be in spirit form."

"What do you mean by read them?" Jeremy enquired.

"I meant see them," Force corrected himself.

"No, you didn't. Are you psychic or something?" Jeremy asked.

"Yeah, or something."

"Are you a fairy too?" Breanna asked him.

"No, I am not a fairy. Why do you kids ask so many questions?"

"He's a vampire. Look at his eyes," Hannah said.

"He's not a vampire," William said rolling his eyes. "He hasn't burst into flames or sparkled like a diamond. He is just a regular guy with contact lenses, aren't you Mister?"

Force thought about lying but remembered he would need to use his powers to sculpt out the tunnel so he could fit through. These kids had already proven they were highly intelligent, and didn't miss a thing. He couldn't let them go through first, not knowing what lay on the other side of the tunnel, and he couldn't push the dirt through to the other side for the same reason. He would have to bring the earth towards him, and store it to the side. There was no way he could do this without the children noticing. They were going to know he was different. He would have to be up front with them, to prevent trouble later.

"I am not a fairy, nor am I a vampire. I am a Gatherer, which is a special kind of Battle Star."

The children began talking over top of one another, and sounded like a babble of indeterminate noises. Force held up his hand to quieten the children, so he could make his explanation quickly. He was pretty sure Scout was close to the other entry point, and he wanted to be ready to go as soon as she entered her end.

"I will give you a quick explanation of what a Gatherer is, but you have to be quiet and not ask any questions." Once he had received their acceptance of the rules, he began his short lesson. "A Battle Star is a human who has been exposed to high amounts of radiation, during a transfer process from this world to another. The traveller's DNA is modified to a point where the human develops the ability to control the five different elements; earth, fire, water, air and spirit."

Force gave them a demonstration of the different things he could do. He created fireballs and waterspouts. He shaped and twisted the earth, until a statue of himself stood before them. Force transformed himself into creatures suggested by the children and he read their minds for real, unlike the magician that had passed through the town a fortnight ago.

The thing that pleased the children most of all, was when he placed his hands on Donovan's body and completely healed his Leukaemia. They couldn't see the changes that had occurred at the cellular level, but when he rolled up his sleeves, they could see the bruises that were usually visible on his arms were gone after Force had touched him. Force told him the next time he went to his oncologist, he would be able to confirm that his disease was completely gone.

Donovan hugged him out of gratitude. He didn't think about it, just launched himself at this stranger who had walked into his life, and changed it forever. He could feel the difference in his body, and couldn't find the words to convey his appreciation for taking the sickness away.

"You haven't passed it on to someone else, have you?" Donovan asked him fearfully.

"No, of course not. Why would you ask that?"

"Because in the movies, when someone cheats death, the reaper takes somebody else in their place. One life for another and all of that," he explained.

"That isn't a real thing. You kids have got to stop watching television shows, and believing they are real. Unless of course they are a documentary, news broadcast, or say 'based on a true story'."

"That statement is hilarious, considering what you just showed us you can do," Jacinta remarked.

Force looked at her and smiled. This one was definitely trouble. He wondered, when Jacinta and Calamity become friends, which one would come out as the 'leader of the pack'. In his long, three thousand and twenty-one years' experience of human relationships, he had discovered there was always one person who rose to the top of the others, to become leader of the group. The others didn't always realise a hierarchy existed, but it was there, nonetheless.

Both girls were head strong. Yes, it would have been very interesting to have the opportunity to watch the dynamics in this group develop. Too bad his job would have him moving on, once the threat from the creatures had been diffused.

Force's connection with Scout told him she had discovered a hidden doorway to the underground cavern. He spoke to the earthen statue of himself, telling it to return to the ground. It exploded theatrically and was there no more.

The children were beside themselves with excitement. This was their best day ever, and they thought they would never forget it. Of course, there would be no memory of any of this left, once Force had finished with them. Occasionally, however, some of the children dreamt of people with super powers that saved children from monsters. These children grew up to lead very interesting lives. He gained the children's attention, and told them it was time to search the creatures' hideout.

"Before we go in, are you able to make sure that William never develops Leukaemia as well?" Donovan asked.

JEALOUSY MONSTERS

"Of course I can, little buddy," Force replied. He placed his hands on William's body and set his healing power to work. William felt tingly from his head to his toes. He hugged his brother for thinking to ask this of Force, then shook Force's hand out of appreciation.

Twenty

Force entered through the doorway first. He warned the children about the rocky, slippery-slide styled entrance.

Breanna and Hannah decided to sit down in the doorway and wiggle forward, until gravity took their bodies down the steep windy path. As they screamed the whole way down, Force wondered if his eardrums would survive another five entries like that one. Even coming down together, they had been terrified.

He was impressed with the acoustics of the cavern. The sound was amplified, and the echoes gave their tones a stereo effect. Jacinta came down next, preferring to lie on her tummy, to enjoy the journey head on. "Weeeee," she squealed. Force placed his pointer fingers in his ears and wiggled them to make them feel better. It didn't work.

Justine was next to enter, and chose to walk down the side of the slope. She took off her shoes, tied them together and lay them over her shoulders, round the back of her neck. Then she took a step inside, and turned around to face the opening.

She crouched low to the ground placing her hands in the dirt. Slowly, she moved her foot backwards until she found the fall in ground level. Moving her hands toward her, Justine pushed her other foot backwards and continued to slowly make her way downwards. Suddenly the gradient changed, and the ground that had been beneath her sliding foot, dropped away. She lost her balance and landed painfully, winding herself. Her body flew down the pathway feet first on her tummy, until she thumped into Force's arms at the bottom.

"Nice and calm. Breathe in deeply," Force said slowly and quietly. He repeated the words until she was able to suck in a lungful of air. "That's it, nice and easy. You'll be all right," he assured her.

Force called up to the boys. One of the twins was going to go next, and he was planning on running all the way to the bottom. "I know what you are thinking and I will not be healing those bones when you break them. If you know what is good for you, you will follow Hannah and Breanna's method, by sitting on your bottom and sliding down properly."

The boys took his advice, not wanting to risk his wrath, and came down carefully. Force was surprised that his little speech had worked. He made sure Justine had recovered, before taking the children into the next section of the cave. "Don't touch the water, it's hot," he told them.

"Look at the drawings on the walls. Where do you think they came from?" Jacinta asked.

"We can't be here. This is the sacred ground of my people!" Justine exclaimed.

"Your people. Do you mean your family?" Jeremy asked.

"Kind of. These are aboriginal paintings done by my people. Sir, we are standing on sacred ground, and we don't have permission from the Elders to be here. We have to leave and ask forgiveness for our disrespect."

"We can't leave, Justine. The creatures have the children down here. I just know it. Once we have them, and the creatures, we can leave."

"I can't stay here. Can't you do your mind thing and see if they really are here," she implored.

"No, my mind waves are blocked down here. I can't sense anything. Let's move quickly so we can respect Justine's, and her people's, heritage. I'll just make this tunnel bigger so I can fit through. Then we will be in another section, and will no longer be disturbing this sacred ground."

"How do you know there is another section beyond this one?" Jacinta questioned.

"Not only can I manipulate the earth to create a statue, I can feel the layout of the land through my skin," he replied.

"How far can you sense?" Jeremy asked.

"A long way!" Force said, sounding angrier than he intended. He was getting frustrated with all the questions thrown at him by these kids when he was so close to finding the kidnapped children.

"You can't change the shape of this place! The spirits will be angry," Justine said, with annoyance.

"Dude, why don't you just turn yourself into a cat or something?" William said.

"Man, how do you ever save kids from creatures on your own?" Donovan asked.

"He has Scout," Jacinta giggled.

Force felt like an idiot. Why hadn't he thought of that? What was wrong with him today? Scout had told him not to go in there because the tunnel was too small. Why was his first thought to make it bigger, rather than himself smaller? He didn't have the answers for any of those questions.

The children were looking to him for leadership, and he was standing there like a nincompoop. He turned himself into a small dog, as he didn't want to follow their suggestion by becoming a cat, and ran into the tunnel. The children didn't follow.

"Come on, kids," Force said, changing his head and throat into that of a human so that he could speak. He made sure they couldn't see him and become frightened.

"It is dark in there," Jeremy whined.

Force changed his head and throat back into a dog's and scampered out of the tunnel. He transformed back into human form and took one of the torches off the wall.

"This is pretty heavy. Which of you wants the responsibility of pushing this into the tunnel, making sure the flame doesn't go out?"

"I will take it," Jacinta said, holding out her hand.

Force transformed into the dog and ran into the tunnel.

The children followed in quick succession.

"Why have we stopped?" Jeremy whined bringing up the rear.

"Dopey, is just standing there, blocking my way," Jacinta answered him.

Force pressed his nose against the opening and felt something hard hindering his advancement. He moved left and he moved right, but couldn't find a way to break through the invisible barrier. Jacinta pushed him and he yelped in pain. Before his neck could break from the unyielding pressure, he transformed himself into a bird.

"Oh," Jacinta grunted.

"What's happening?" Jeremy whined again. He was claustrophobic and wanted to get the ordeal over and done with.

JEALOUSY MONSTERS

Force couldn't speak in his current state so he entered Jacinta's mind and placed a thought there for her to interpret.

"He can't get through. There seems to be some sort of barrier in the way."

"What does it feel like?" Justine asked, thinking the spirits were angry.

"Hang on a sec, I'll have a look."

She wriggled forward and reached out her hand. It went right through the opening. She wriggled forward a bit more and her head poked through, followed by her torso and legs. On the other side, she got up on her hands and knees and looked back down the tunnel.

"There's nothing there. He must have been trying to scare us. Come on through."

Force tried to follow Jacinta but was stopped once again. He tried to fly and crashed, fluttering to the ground. He hopped twice on his legs and hit the barrier, flopping over to one side. Justine watched his attempts and frowned. She picked him up in her hands and gently stroked his feathers.

"Are you okay, little bird?" she asked him. "Maybe the spirits won't allow animals to enter the new place. After we have gone through, you should turn yourself into a child. Perhaps then the spirits will grant you entry." She let him go and wriggled forward until she was able to stand alongside Jacinta.

One after the other, the children entered the white room, which was currently empty. Jacinta leaned down and called to Force. He had turned himself into a younger version of himself but was still unable to get through the barrier. She tried to put her hand through to give him some help, and was surprised to feel a hard surface beneath her fingertips. She moved her hand around to find a gap but there was none.

"I can't get through," she told Force.

"Neither can I," he replied. '*At least we can still communicate,*' he thought. "What do you see?"

"It's a room with white walls, ceiling and a concrete floor," Jacinta told him.

"What are the walls and ceiling made of?"

"I think they are concrete too," she said running her hands over the smooth, cool surface.

"Can you see any windows or doorways?"

"No," she said in a panicked tone.

"There seems to be a gap over here, look," Hannah said.

The children walked over to where Hannah indicated, and saw there was a very slim, rectangular border around a section of the wall. There didn't seem to be a handle to pull down, or turn, so they pushed on the surface as hard as they could. Nothing happened.

"Mister, we can see what looks like a doorway, but don't know how to open it," Jacinta said.

"Kids, my name is Force. Please use it. See if you can find something else."

The children separated into two groups. The first group went left, and began searching the surface for discrepancies. The second group went right. By the time they met again on the other side of the room, they were back at the tunnel and had not found another exit.

"This is hopeless," Jeremy moaned. He wished he was back at the park pushing the girls on the swings. "I should never have followed you all."

"This is a fantastic adventure, Jeremy," Breanna said to him. "Do you know how much our parents would love for something like this to happen to them? Have you never listened to them when something interferes with their everyday routine? It's like they are a puppet on a string, waiting for their puppeteer to come along and animate them. When that happens, they come alive. They talk excitedly, moving from one house to the next, telling their neighbours what happened, and embellishing the story with each recount."

Hannah decided to join in the conversation. "We have been presented with an opportunity to help save a bunch of kids, just like us. We shouldn't become disheartened just because it has become a bit hard. Nothing worth having ever comes easy."

"It takes a lot of elbow grease and hard work. At least that's what our dad says," William added sheepishly.

"Yeah, but your dad is a mechanic," replied Jeremy.

"You are missing the point," Force interjected. "Your friends are trying to help you realise it is okay to be scared, as long as you don't let that fear rule your decisions. Do you think you can give them a hand to find a way out of this predicament?"

"I don't know," he mumbled.

"Oh, for heaven's sake, Jeremy. Snap out of it! Are you a man or a mouse?" Jacinta yelled at him.

"I'm a boy," he said a bit more forcefully.

"Are you really, or are you a girl in boys clothing?"

"I am a boy," he said louder.

"And what are you going to do to prove you are a boy, soldier?"

"I am going to find a way to open that door over there, Ma'am, um, Jacinta."

229

"Thank you, Jeremy," she said with quiet sincerity.

He walked to the other side and lightly ran his hands over the wall inside the border. His fingers felt a few bumps that his eyes couldn't see. He pressed his finger firmly on the raised part in the middle, and the wall they had been looking at disappeared. Seated before them, were the six missing children.

Twenty-One

"Jeremy, you did it," the children chorused.

"The wall is still here, we just can't see it," he mentioned, before someone hurt themselves trying to step through.

The children on the other side looked absolutely miserable. Three girls and three boys either lay on the floor with their head on their arm, or were sitting cross-legged with their head in their hands. Their clothes had been taken away and replaced with a singlet and pair of underpants. Physically, they looked to be in good health, their postures, however, told a different story. The rescuers bashed on the wall but the missing kids never reacted.

"They can't hear us!" Jeremy moaned.

"Do something else," Jacinta encouraged him.

"Like what?"

"I don't know, like what you did before," she suggested.

He ran his hands further along and found the next bump. He pushed that, and the wall split right down the middle, and slid in opposite directions. The noise was intense, as the walls moved along big, steel runners. The children on the other side jumped up in fright. They watched the walls, which still looked like white concrete from their side, move.

Force cautioned his kids to be careful. The children before them had been in the hands of monsters for at least a month, and they would be frightened, and untrusting of what their eyes told them was there. The gap widened enough for the children on the other side to see they had visitors. The one who had been taken first, Geoffrey, moved forward in a protective gesture of his fellow captives.

He wasn't the tallest of the group, but was definitely the one that exuded leadership qualities in spades. The brown of his irises was so dark, his eyes appeared almost black, and gave a creepy vibe. His sun-bleached hair was longer and shaggier than he normally wore it, but it suited him. The thing that stood out most about Geoffrey, and the other children that had been taken, was how white their skin had become. Even Michael, who had been the last to be taken, was whiter than the twins who were the palest in Calamity's group. Jacinta placed herself inside the widening gap in the walls.

"Hello, my name is Jacinta."

"Geoffrey."

"These are my friends. We have come to find our friend Calamity. Is she in there with you?"

"No, she is not."

"Have you seen her? She has very dark red hair."

"We have seen her," he said cutting Jacinta off. "She is off somewhere with Lucas and Ruby."

"You don't seem to like her."

"You got that right. Why don't you guys leave the way you came? You are not wanted here."

"Geoffrey, Geoffrey's friends, your parents are missing you something fierce. We can help you get home. We've got a guy inside that can help."

"You can get me home?" Michael questioned.

"Yes, we can. Are you ready to go home?"

"Yes," he answered and burst into tears.

Jacinta stepped forward, but Geoffrey blocked her way. Michael pushed him aside, and grabbed Jacinta's hand. Belinda stepped forward next, then the other three moved, too.

"Are you all ready to go home? Can you get through the tunnel over there?"

"No, there is a barrier we can't break through."

"Try again," Jeremy suggested, pushing the third bump.

Michael ran over to the tunnel and touched the surface of the entrance. His hand went straight through. He pushed his arm in all the way to his shoulder. With a sob of relief, he climbed into the tunnel. Force wriggled backward and Michael wriggled forward. They made it to the other end of the tunnel, together. All of the other missing children, except Geoffrey, climbed into the tunnel and followed.

"You can go home, Geoffrey," Jacinta encouraged.

"I don't have anything to go home to. My parents are dead, and my foster parents couldn't give a damn."

"My parents would take you in. You could come and live with me." Jacinta said.

Geoffrey laughed. "That is the stupidest thing I have ever heard."

"It's true. They have fostered kids before."

"And where are they now?"

"Back with *their* parents. But *you* wouldn't have to leave. You could be my brother forever if you wanted to be." Jacinta's new friends listened to her with unbelieving ears. She was either the world's biggest liar, or the world's greatest saint.

"I don't know," he said.

"Geoffrey, all you have to do is climb into that tunnel, and trust in our friend on the other side. His name is Force, and he will take care of you. He's got contacts, and my parents will be back at dinner time," Jacinta told him.

Geoffrey didn't trust her, but didn't want to stay with Ruby and Lucas either. He walked over to the tunnel and without looking back, shuffled his way through. Force told his kids to try again to break through the barrier. Jeremy walked to the tunnel, and placed his hand through the entrance.

"It's open," he happily reported and crawled through after the missing children. Breanna, Hannah, Justine and the two boys followed, but when it was Jacinta's turn to climb in, the tunnel shut her out.

"Let me in," she told the tunnel. It refused. "Please tunnel, let me come in." No, the barrier stood intact.

"Are you coming, Jacinta?" Force asked after the others had appeared at his end.

"I can't get through!" she yelled to him. "Take the others to safety. Then please come back for me."

"I can't leave you here. Has Scout arrived yet?"

"No," Jacinta replied, after a quick scan of the room. "She can't be too far away. Surely this place can't be that big. Go on, I'll be okay."

"I'll be back as soon as I can," Force said.

"I know. I'll be here."

'I hope so,' Force thought.

Jacinta could hear him mumbling directions to the kids. She wondered how they were going to climb the steep hill in the first section they had entered. She knew Force was pretty resourceful and would come up with some awe-inspiring solution, if he wasn't being a Dopey. Jacinta thought she should check out the other room to see if she could find the exit, when she spotted Calamity standing there, staring at her.

"Hello, Jacinta, fancy seeing you here."

"Calamity, are you all right? Where have you been? Where are Ruby and Lucas? Are they with you?"

Calamity just stared at her. She didn't answer any of her questions and Jacinta, being wise, stopped asking them. She figured Calamity would speak to her when she was ready, and obviously, that time was not now. Jacinta decided to save her energy and sat on the floor. She knew it would be at least a few hours before Force came back for her.

Until Scout showed up, she would be more than happy to play the waiting game. Calamity didn't know the others had escaped, did she? It wasn't something Jacinta could ask, so she waited to see if Calamity mentioned them at all.

"I guess you are wondering why I am here?" Calamity asked her.

"Sure, why are you here?"

"I've come to show you something. Say hello to my new pet. Her name is Flutter."

Calamity stepped left and picked something up off the ground. She held up a bird cage for Jacinta to see. Trapped inside was her newest friend, Scout.

"Scout, are you okay?"

"I am fine, Jacinta. Just annoyed at getting caught," Scout replied, unable to be heard.

"Her name is Flutter, Jacinta! Enjoy each other while you can. Everything will change when Lucas and Ruby return," Calamity informed them.

She placed the cage in front of Jacinta, and walked out of the room, and into the one the missing children had been held in. Jacinta tried to tell Calamity that Lucas and Ruby were evil, but of course Calamity wouldn't listen to a word she said. Calamity was totally blinded by jealousy.

It would take somebody else to awaken Calamity from the hold the pair had over her. There was no way Jacinta was going to be able to make Calamity lose the jealous feelings she felt towards her. Only a third party would be able to get through to her, and make her realise there was no reason for Calamity to feel jealous of Jacinta. Calamity had a pretty good life. She just needed someone, other than Jacinta, to point that out to her.

Twenty-Two

Jacinta was as frustrated by the cage, as she was by the room she had become imprisoned in. She couldn't find a way to open the door on either. Scout grabbed hold of the bars and tried to rattle them. They wouldn't budge. She tried to kick open the door. It wouldn't move.

Both of them were at a loss as to how this particular bird cage worked. There was no pin holding it closed, neither was there a padlock on the door. The door did not have a keyhole nor did it have a number pad. Scout had not actually seen how they had opened the door to put her in there. She had been blinded by the finger that had been placed over her face when she had been plucked from the air.

Scout had not been alert enough to see the shimmer of Lucas' essence as she flew past. Then all of a sudden, a hand had materialised out of thin air and wrapped itself around her body. Next thing she knew, she was stuck in a bird cage and her magic was on the fritz.

Jacinta apologised to Scout for getting her into this mess. Scout assured Jacinta she had nothing to do with her getting caught. At Jacinta's prompting, she decided to tell her a story. They had time on their hands, and Scout was pretty sure Force was going to wipe Jacinta's memory anyway, if they managed to make it out of this ordeal alive. Besides, she could see Jacinta had been touched by the hand of fate, and was going to have a very interesting career.

"Jacinta, there are a multitude of hidden worlds that you humans are not quite evolved enough to fathom. There was a time when humans were at the bottom of the food chain, and were preyed upon by the most terrifying creatures no child could ever have imagined. For many millennia, creatures from other realms viewed the Earth in a similar fashion to a popular takeaway shop. As a result, the human race never had the opportunity to flourish and evolve into the beings they were designed to become.

"Three millennia ago, a new planet was created in a faraway universe, with the intention of saving the human race from the possibility of extinction. The creators took a small group of humans, and transported them to this new world for genetic modification and training. The humans, with their new super powers, were returned to Earth to capture the monsters decimating the human population, and relocate them to the new planet. The Earth was purged of every creature the Battle Stars, the name given to the super-humans, could capture.

"The removal of predation of humans has seen an explosion in population. Thanks to us, the biggest threat to your numbers these days, is yourselves. No longer are you hunted by legions of vampires, werewolves, goblins and the like. The creatures imprisoned on the new planet are superior predators, way more evolved than humans. Even through the natural evolutionary process, it was decided by the Universal Governing Committee, that it was unlikely humans would ever develop an ability to protect themselves from such beasts.

"Humans are a delicacy for most of the species on Mystique, and are viewed as a food source only. Creatures, like vampires and werewolves, occasionally increased their numbers by turning a human, but, unlike the movies and books produced today, this was not as a result of a love affair between the human and the creature.

JEALOUSY MONSTERS

"The change was effected as a result of the unfortunate human's DNA strands reacting to the viruses carried by the creatures in a metamorphic way. Even after three thousand years, we are still living on this planet, protecting humans from creatures they have not developed a defence against."

"Are you telling me you are over three thousand years old?" Jacinta asked her.

"I am three thousand, four hundred and thirty-five years old," she answered.

"Whoa. Were you born or brought here?"

"I was brought here with the other Locators. I used to live in Fairyland."

"Whereabouts is that?"

"We used to be part of the Grandiosma Galaxy, but our land was somehow sucked into the Sxyphonian Universe during the creation of Mystique. It is now incorporated into one of its land masses, amongst the creatures."

"What is Fairyland like?"

"Fairyland is the most beautiful place I have ever seen. It is filled with colours so mesmerising, the human mind is simply incapable of fathoming their existence."

"Like the lights the church committee decorate our town with at Christmas time."

"Oh, Jacinta, it is way prettier than that. It is a shame that you will never know how truly beautiful the universe can be. Your human eyes are just not capable of interpreting the array of colours that exist on the spectrum. Your planet is so plain compared to some of the other planets that exist in space."

"Do you live in houses in Fairyland? Actually, where do you live here?"

"Yes, we live in houses in Fairyland, but they are not like those you build here. Our homes are similar to your mushroom rings and are grouped together in communities. Every fairy has a position within the community they live in and works for the benefit of the group.

"Whilst on Earth, I live in the hollow of a tree I found in one of your mountain ranges. It looked the right size and height to be safe from discovery by you humans. On the floor was some soft moss and feathers, and it was dry. I used broken, clear plastic cups to make window coverings for the assorted holes in the trunk and a door to keep out the rain. It isn't the same as what I had in Fairyland, but it is my home."

"Which mountain range?"

"Not one close enough for you to visit, Jacinta."

"Do you have other fairies living with you?"

"No, we don't live in communities here. We are always on the job looking for our next creature that requires relocation."

"What about between jobs?"

"Like I said, we are always on the job. There are times when I am not physically honing in on the exact location of a creature, but other Locators would be. Living in a community would hinder our abilities. Until we are no longer needed on Earth, we live on our own, and communicate only with our Gatherers."

"You are communicating with me."

"Yes, but this case has been different from the beginning."

"How does your magic work?"

"Fairy dust."

"How does the fairy dust work?"

"Magic."

"Where do you get it from?"

"Gee, you want to know all of my secrets, don't you?"

"I'm sorry, it's not like I was going to tell anybody," Jacinta said sadly.

"We fairies make the fairy dust. When we are truly happy, our singing or dancing stimulates a gland in our body that produces the dust with magical properties. It is then passed through to our Integumentary System and comes out through our pores."

"I see," said Jacinta getting to her feet. "Did you hear that?"

"Yes, I heard that," Lucas said walking into the room with Calamity. "You did a real good job, Cal," he told Calamity as Jacinta's form transformed into Ruby's. Scout got to her feet, unsure of what her eyes were telling her. "I didn't think you had it in you, Kiddo."

"I just did what you told me to do; concentrated on the girl I wanted punished."

Scout was more saddened by what Calamity had said, than the fact that she had just spilled all of her secrets to the creature before her. She worried that Calamity might be too far gone for them to recover her humanity. Perhaps she would become one of those people who were in and out of prison for the rest of their lives. Ruby picked up the cage and left the room with Lucas and Calamity. Through the winding tunnels they went, until they arrived at another open cavernous room.

Twenty-Three

The first thing Scout noticed was that the walls and ceiling were covered in little white lights, similar to the sparkling stars in the sky on a cloudless night. They twinkled on and off at different times to one another, creating an enchanting setting for whatever was to come. As her cage swung towards one of the walls, she realised they were glow worms.

JEALOUSY MONSTERS

Ruby placed her in the middle of a two metre by four metre table, which had been covered with a black table-cloth. There were no chairs surrounding the table, so she assumed they were not about to conduct a meeting, or sit down to a meal. Lucas walked to the eastern wall, and picked something up off a sideboard that had been painted black, and blended into the background.

As he returned, Scout could see that he held a bouquet of pink and purple flowers, with white ribbon woven between the greenery holding it together. He placed the bouquet at the foot of her cage, and walked to the western wall where he picked up another object. Scout turned around to follow his movement, and wondered why he hadn't placed everything he wanted in the same place.

She assumed it was to add drama to the situation. Was he trying to scare her? Well, it wasn't working. He brought a very sharp looking knife, made from the finest silver, back with him. It reminded her of the ceremonial blades the ancients had used to sacrifice their young to the Gods in an attempt to gain immortality.

The handle was moulded into a couple of snakes that had twisted around one another, in their own kind of ritual. Tied to the handle was a ribbon that had once been white, but now looked and smelled of old blood. Okay, now Scout was beginning to worry a bit. She glanced at Calamity to gauge the young girl's reaction to Lucas' preparations.

Calamity stood still, as if in a trance. Her eyes didn't follow his movements, they just stared straight ahead. Her breathing was slow and deep. She didn't appear to be aware of anything that was happening around her. Lucas stepped back from the table, and placed his arms behind his back, as he waited for Ruby to gather her necessities.

She walked to the northern wall and collected a small bag made from golden lace, which had once held Calamity's favourite bracelet. It had since been stuffed with an assortment of herbs and spices, and tied closed with a dark blue ribbon. She laid that beside the knife, and sauntered over to the southern wall. Ruby grabbed the bucket of warm water she had gathered earlier from the pool in the second room and brought it back to the table. She began stripping the petals from the bouquet, and dropped them in the water.

As the petals hit the surface, the sweet aroma of nature was released into the room causing Scout's head to swim with dizziness. She peered at the monsters and then beyond. Jacinta's face swam into view.

"Jacinta, don't let them hurt her!" Scout yelled, before collapsing in a heap on the cage floor.

Ruby chuckled, "She's hallucinating already."

"You did well, my dear. This concoction is going to be pretty potent," he remarked.

Lucas took the little bag from the table and untied the ribbon. He sprinkled the contents over the petals as he chanted in an ancient language. The ceiling transformed into a place of beauty. Plants sprouted out of thin air and

253

produced tendrils filled with delicate flowers, the same colours as those in the bouquet. The lights twinkled merrily between the leaves, giving the illusion of dewdrops glistening in the morning sun.

Scout opened her eyes and her spirit shone with pleasure at the picture before her. She imagined she was home in Fairyland, surrounded by her family and friends. Music drifted to her ears, and the fairies she imagined were around her, began to dance. Scout stood gracefully and began to rock backwards and forwards to the rhythm.

Her feet began to shuffle and she danced in a small circle. Her arms came up in front of her as though she had just been joined by a partner, and her movements became more pronounced. Soon she twirled around her cage in an old fashioned waltz.

The music ended and she stood still, waiting. A new, more upbeat piece began to play. Scout strutted around the cage as though it was her stage, and she was the star, entertaining her fans.

The rhythm increased again, and she began to twerk, then crumped it out. Fairy dust flew everywhere. The monsters had done it! Very soon, they would be flesh and blood and, with any luck, totally immortal.

"Ladies first," Lucas said handing Ruby the knife.

She accepted the ceremonial implement and dipped it in the bucket, before taking hold of Calamity's hand. She placed the blade on Calamity's palm, and gently pressed down as she pulled it towards herself. Ruby ensured the blade was coated in blood before opening the door of the cage and giving it a second coat with fairy dust. She flicked her tongue along the side of the blade until it was clean and handed it to Lucas.

The feeling was instant and incredible. It was like the deep itch that you sometimes feel, deep within your body, but can't scratch. She watched as her essence materialised into flesh.

She pressed one hand against the other and felt the unyielding pressure that came from being solid. Ruby encouraged Lucas to begin his transformation. He followed the steps she had taken, using Calamity's other palm, and soon felt the same sensation Ruby had felt.

They tingled from head to toe until the conversion processes had been completed. Touching each other's face for the first time, they were startled by the feelings of desire that assaulted their senses. They were so confused by their new feelings, they didn't see the real Jacinta enter the room.

Twenty-Four

Jacinta snuck past them, and checked on Scout first. She was still under their spell, dancing to the music that only she could hear. Jacinta carefully reached her hand in through the opening of the cage, and gently touched Scout on the arm. The physical contact with another being was enough to undo the enchantment, and bring her back to reality.

Scout was annoyed to see Jacinta standing before her, as she thought it was Ruby. She squinted when Jacinta placed her finger up to her lips in the universal sign of 'silence'. *What the hell is she doing?*' Scout thought.

Jacinta pointed behind her, drawing Scout's eyes. Her eyebrows rose involuntarily, as she witnessed the affectionate behaviour the creatures were displaying towards one another. Her mind registered the fact that the creatures had crossed over to the physical realm. They no longer looked exactly like the Lucas and Ruby she was used to seeing. They looked like the monsters they had always been, but had been able to mask, so as not to scare the children they interacted with. She looked to Jacinta for an explanation.

Jacinta raised her arms and created little flapping motions with her hands, then pointed to the place where she had entered the room. Scout nodded her head and took a couple of steps, before pointing to Calamity. Jacinta indicated she would take care of Calamity, by pointing to herself. Jacinta pointed to Scout, and then the door again. Scout checked that the creatures were still unaware of Jacinta's presence, before taking flight.

Jacinta watched her leave safely, and then turned her attention to Calamity. She waved her hands in front of Calamity's face, but out of sight of the creatures. She didn't want to alert them to her presence, but then, she didn't really want Calamity to see her, and make a scene either.

Calamity didn't react to her movements at all. Jacinta grabbed her by the hand, and held in the 'ugh' that threatened to escape her throat. It felt wet and sticky. She rolled it over to have a look. Blood had begun to coagulate from the long, straight cut on her palm. 'That must hurt a lot,' Jacinta thought, yet Calamity had not reacted in any way at all. "What have they done to you?" she whispered beneath her breath.

Jacinta re-gripped, this time around her wrist, and coaxed her out the door. Calamity stepped one foot in front of the other, without actually seeing or thinking about what she was doing. She was simply being led along. Once the pair had managed to make it out of the room unseen, Scout told Jacinta she had found her bearings, and knew the way back to the entrance she had located in the forest.

Jacinta asked her to take Calamity to the forest, and wait for her there. Scout refused to leave without her, so they travelled to the forest together. Once they were out of the cave system, Scout and Jacinta had a quick conversation.

"Jacinta, how did you get away from the other kids, and come in the same way I did?"

"It's a long story that we don't have time for now."

"Yes, we do. You need to tell me how you did that!"

"I was with the other kids at the swing when Lucas spoke to us. He disappeared behind a tree. I told the others to wait and I went into the woods to look for him. I found his trail so went back to where I left them and I saw you talking to me and the others."

"Did you just say you saw yourself?"

"Yes, at the swing. You were talking to a girl that looked like me, but wasn't me."

"I'll be damned. She was running a scam for my benefit, way back then."

"Scout, they needed your magic dust to become tangible."

"Why would they want to be?"

"It takes a lot of power to keep them in existence. If they became real, the power they drained from the children could be diverted into evilness, rather than keeping them alive. They plan on creating environments, in which feelings of jealousy will overtake every other emotion, thereby creating more creatures like them. Then, by catching fairies like you, they could help the newly created essences materialise into flesh and blood, making them even more terrifying," explained Jacinta.

"I actually think they are scarier as spirits."

"No, I don't agree. I am more frightened of them now that they are real and can wield knives and other weapons," Jacinta said.

"How do you know all of this?"

"I have been listening to them hatching their plans. I needed to wait until they became real, before I could put my plan into action," she said.

"What is your plan, Jacinta?"

"To dip the knife in the bucket, put my blood, that of a non-jealous person, on the knife and dip it into your fairy dust."

"And then what?" Scout questioned.

"I don't know. Jab them with it," Jacinta suggested.

"No, you can't do that. There are two of them. You will never get them both."

"What else can we do?"

"We can wait for Force. They are real now. His powers will work on them, and he can get the Collectors to come and take them away. He could be a few hours, though. How are we going to keep them here until then?"

"You will have to go back in there, Scout. They won't harm you, and you and Force seem to have that special connection, that will allow him to find and rescue you. Besides, I will be able to show him where to start looking."

"You are a gem, Jacinta."

"What about Calamity? Is she going to be okay?"

"Force will take care of her. Now I need you to be a beacon. I want you to say Force's name in your head, every thirty seconds. When he is able, he will pick up on that thought, and it will guide him right to you."

"Cool," Jacinta replied.

Scout flew back inside the cave, and zigzagged her way back to the creatures. She was amazed to discover they had still not noticed her disappearance. She placed herself back in the cage, arranged herself on the floor, and pretended to be asleep.

'Force.'

Ruby and Lucas felt the first pangs of hunger and didn't know what it meant. Ruby grabbed her tummy and rubbed. Lucas suddenly doubled over like he was going to throw up, and moaned in agony.

'Force.'

"What is happening to us!" he screamed.

Scout stretched as if waking from a dream, and rubbed her eyes with her fists. She half sat and half lay, as she asked him to repeat what he said.

"Ow," he groaned with pain.

"Aaaah," Ruby joined in.

'Force.'

"It looks like you are hungry. What do you eat?" Scout asked them with interest.

"What do we eat?" Ruby asked Lucas.

"I don't know," he grumbled. "Where is Cal?" he asked Ruby.

She spun around in a circle but couldn't see her anywhere in the room. "She's gone."

'Force.'

"Find her!" he yelled at her.

"Wait," Ruby cautioned. "Can you feel it?" she asked with surprise.

JEALOUSY MONSTERS

Lucas stilled himself and concentrated. After a few seconds, it came to him. "Well, well, well. Who might we be jealous of?" he questioned Scout.

"I'm not jealous!"

Ruby and Lucas laughed at her vehemence. Of course she had feelings of jealousy, though she was so adamant that she didn't. They stepped towards her, and she backed herself up until she hit the bars at the back of the cage. She was trapped, nowhere to go.

Twenty-Five

Scout attempted to clear her mind of everything, and to replace the emptiness with positive thoughts. She knew the mind couldn't simply think of nothing. It was too powerful a machine. There was always something going on in the subconscious mind.

The more she tried to be positive, the more her mind zeroed in on their statement, and focused on Force's kiss with Loretta. They absorbed the waves of jealousy that seeped from the pores in her skin. Their hunger pains were soothed as they fed off Scout, but then a new pain assaulted them.

Their legs suddenly felt like they were being constricted by a carpet snake. They looked down and saw a golden mist wrapped around the lower half of their bodies. Ruby tried to escape, and felt it tightening across her skin. Lucas attempted to jump up on to the table, but found he couldn't even get his feet off the ground.

"Yeah, that's right," Scout told them throwing her arms in the air, and spreading her fingers like a cool dude. "My Gatherer has just busted your sorry butts."

Force stepped into view and said, "Lucas and Ruby, you have been found guilty of carrying on business that adversely affects the humans on this planet. You will be relocated to the planet, Mystique, to carry out your sentence. There will be no parole period, and your sentence will be for the remainder of your lifespan. A Collector will be here shortly to carry out the transfer."

Jacinta, who had been watching and listening asked, "Is that it? Man, what a letdown."

Force spun to face her and pressed his lips together. It shouldn't have surprised him that Jacinta would not be content to stay in the forest with Calamity. While he acknowledged she would probably make a great Battle Star one day, he was annoyed that she had taken it on herself to sneak back inside the cavern where the danger lay.

"Our job is not always bells and whistles. In fact, it is better when there aren't any. Less cleaning up for me to deal with. You'll understand one day," Force replied.

"What does that mean?"

"Guardian Karah," Scout said as a woman walked into the room.

She was beautiful. Tall, thin and lithe, she exuded confidence and grace befitting that of the Queen's right hand lady. Her tender, brown eyes held Scout's as she smiled in warm greeting. Her orange coloured hair fell gently across her shoulders, providing a beautiful contrast to her dark grey and aquamarine coloured jacket that indicated the wearer was a Guardian in the royal court. Her dark grey pants hugged her legs like a second skin and finished inside her dark grey and aquamarine boots that completed her uniform. "Hey there, Scout, great job in finding these two."

"Thank you, Ma'am," Scout said with pride.

"I wish you wouldn't call me that. Guardian will do. These two are going to be major trouble back home," Karah told them. "There is a lot of competition amongst the Battle Stars at the moment, which is breeding a great deal of jealousy. You might want to keep your eyes peeled for future trouble in this area, Scout. There could be more instances of this type of creature, with trips to Earth becoming a more frequent necessity."

"Are we having a spike in the number of creatures?" Force asked her.

"You have no idea. I need to get these two home and settled in, but I'll be back in a couple of hours to deal with the other issue we discussed," she said, flicking her eyes towards Jacinta. "See you then?"

"Sure."

Scout wanted to ask how the guardian had managed to get there so quickly, and what issue she had to deal with, but didn't. Guardian Karah could have her reassigned, or worse; sent back home, while there was still work to be done here. She watched the guardian take control over the mist, and levitate the creatures to the exit. They screamed with rage, but were unable to escape. They were going on a one way trip.

Force, Scout, and Jacinta left the cavern and found Calamity, who was still under the influence of the Jealousy Monsters, sitting in the same place Jacinta had left her. Scout asked Force what Karah had been talking about, but he didn't want to discuss the matter in front of Jacinta. They left the forest and walked out into the open, where Jacinta worked out it was probably around five o'clock in the afternoon.

Force and Scout picked up on Jacinta's mood and Scout asked her, "Are you still upset by how easily Force captured the creatures?"

"My parents will be arriving home soon, if they're not already, and are going to be angry or worried or both."

Force said, "Remember when I told you I had called in a favour with one of my Gatherer buddies so she could take care of the children, and I could come back here to help you more quickly? She caught up with your parents, and told them you were instrumental in finding the missing children, and that you were still helping us with our investigation."

"Oh, shoot. They are really going to be worried. Why did you do that?"

"Jacinta, your parents were so proud when she told them. They do not believe you are in any danger now. April made sure of that. You will not be in any kind of trouble when you get home. In fact, I wouldn't be shocked if they didn't have a surprise for you."

"Really?"

"Really. Now, do you want to walk for an hour, or would you like to ride a dragon, or a unicorn, or something else your heart desires."

Jacinta took her time in thinking about the offer he had given her. As exciting as all of those things would be, she knew the last thing they would want to do is draw attention to themselves. Besides, he and Scout would be moving on to their next job, now that the danger had been neutralised here. She wanted to spend as much time with them as possible before they left, and because of Calamity's condition, she wouldn't be able to ride any of these creatures

"I would like to walk home with you both," she told him. "What are we going to do about Calamity?"

"Force will heal her hands now, so they don't get infected, but we will get you home before he gives her any kind of therapy. She will be a different, happier person when he is through with her," Scout advised.

"You're not going to change her personality, are you?" Jacinta questioned.

"Of course not. We can't change the fundamental make up of a person. I can make her appreciate what she has though, and make her more susceptible to positive influences, such as yourself," he told her. "Ready to go?"

Jacinta nodded, took Calamity by the healed hand, and then headed off.

Twenty-Six

During their long walk to town, they gave Jacinta the opportunity to discuss the events that had occurred during the past twelve hours.

Jacinta started with how sad she had been that morning, when Calamity had turned up at the river, and picked a fight with her. For the first time since moving to the town, she had actually been frightened of Calamity. Then Jacinta expressed her enjoyment at seeing Calamity's face drop when Scout had turned up, full-sized, and invited her to a non-existent party.

She wasn't sure how she felt about discovering there were real monsters in the world, with fairies and super-humans hunting them for capture and relocation. Jacinta had never been a child who was afraid of the dark, or scared to walk down the street on her own. Thanks to recent events, there had been a mammoth shift in her perception of the world. She wondered if she would have trouble going to sleep tonight, or think twice about going to the park or river in the morning.

She knew she wouldn't look at the hills the same way. Even knowing that Ruby and Lucas were no longer there, she was unsure whether she would venture there again without the others.

Force and Scout listened to her without saying a word. They knew she would not remember any of this before she went to bed, and would have no problems falling asleep. Neither would she be afraid to play at the park, river, or in the hills on her own.

As a Gatherer, Force was not allowed to let any human, who had not been targeted by a creature, to keep any knowledge of such things. She would not have any memories of Ruby and Lucas as monsters. They would simply be remembered as two wayward teenagers who had kidnapped six children, and gotten caught, with her help, in the process of trying to take Calamity as their seventh.

If he had his way, he would leave small tendrils in Jacinta's brain to nudge her mind into being open to strange possibilities. Then he would erase her memories to the point where they became translucent, rather than non-existent, so they would appear to be dreamlike.

He had developed a soft spot for Jacinta, and didn't want her to forget him or Scout.

Unfortunately, the task of tampering with Jacinta's memories had been taken out of his hands.

Jacinta was destined, and as such, it was a guardian's task to shape her memories so that, when the time came, she would be ready to fulfil her role in the universe. That is why Guardian Karah would be returning in a couple of hours. Force wished he could stick around a few years, to watch the opportunity that lay ahead of her unfold. He knew that just wasn't possible.

His purpose was to protect the humans, and he couldn't sacrifice those in need of his help, for his own selfish reasons. The best he could hope for was being given the opportunity to play a further part in her destiny. Perhaps he would be the one chosen to open the portal for her when the time came.

Jacinta talked about her feelings when she came out of the woods, and saw the children at the swing. She had wanted to come out of hiding so badly, but couldn't after she had seen Ruby impersonating her. The last thing she had wanted to do was scare the children she was trying to be friends with, and show them there was some serious magic going on in their town.

It had been so hard for her to decide to leave the children, and follow Lucas. She couldn't explain to them why she had chosen that course. Even though she would have been exposed to a certain extent while following the kids, and they may have spotted her, that wasn't the reason she chose to go in the other direction. Nor was it because she wanted to be a hero, and save Calamity from the creatures herself.

She had, however, been pleased with her decision in the end, as it had enabled her to help Scout and Calamity escape from the room. Then she explained how sad she had felt when asking Scout to return to the ceremonial chamber, as a diversionary tactic until Force could return to save Scout and Calamity.

Scout appreciated Jacinta's sentiments, and revealed her wish that they could have become friends. Jacinta was gutted to think that they were not already friends, and that Scout had no desire to make her wish become a reality. Scout wanted to clear the air and explain that Jacinta had misunderstood her. Force entered Scout's mind and told her to leave it be. There was no point in raising Jacinta's hopes, he told her, when her mind was going to be blanked anyway.

Scout disagreed, and went to clarify her previous statement, but didn't want to bring up the subject of mind erasure. Instead, she simply stated that her work would take her far away from Jacinta, and it would be hard to keep in contact with one another.

Jacinta felt better, and continued with her monologue. Scout was becoming tired and wanted to save her energy for the flight home. Instead of settling on Force's shoulder, she chose to land on Jacinta's, to reinforce the genuine feelings she felt for the girl.

Jacinta told her how she had followed Lucas into the cavern, and how she had watched him put the bouquet together. He had pulled the knife out of a velvet covered box, and whispered words she didn't understand.

He tied a ribbon around the handle, and raised it above his head. Then he took the bouquet and knife, and placed them along the walls in the sparkled chamber. She told them how fast her heart had been beating, and how worried she had been for Calamity. Then he turned around and nearly spotted her. She thought her heart was going to stop beating from fear. That was when she spotted Scout in the cage. Jacinta hadn't even known Scout had been captured.

Calamity stumbled and Force held out his hand to steady her. Jacinta stopped talking and stared at her with excitement and fear. How would Calamity react when she came out of her stupor, and saw Jacinta walking beside her?

Did this mean she was going to be okay, and whatever they had done to her was wearing off? Force delved inside Calamity's mind, and found the connections to her consciousness were beginning to fire.

JEALOUSY MONSTERS

"Guardian Karah has left the planet with Ruby and Lucas. Their hold over Calamity has been severed, and she is beginning to waken from whatever nightmare she has been trapped inside of," he told them.

"What can we do to help her?" Jacinta asked.

"Be a good friend to her whether she deserves it or not," Scout replied. "It will go a long way in her healing process."

"I have always wanted to be her friend," Jacinta remarked.

"Mum," Calamity spoke.

Force sat her down on the ground, and held her hands to keep her physical-self calm while he changed her memories. He tapped Jacinta in, so she wouldn't say anything confusing to Calamity for the rest of the journey home.

"*Calamity, my name is Liam Force, but everybody just calls me Force. I am a private investigator who has been looking into the disappearance of missing children in the area. During the investigation, I discovered, with the help of your friend, Jacinta, that there were a* couple of teenagers named Lucas and Ruby, who had been lurking around this area for the past two to three weeks.

"Unfortunately, they were able to lure you away before we could stop them. After taking you inside the cave, you went into shock and don't remember anything until Jacinta found you, and helped you escape. I caught the baddies and handed them over to federal agents. Then we began walking home together."

Force severed the connection between himself, Calamity and Jacinta. He asked Scout to fly inside his pocket so he could bring Calamity out of her daydream-like-slumber. Normally, Calamity would be forced to remember the monsters because she was targeted by them, but these monsters were different to the usual ones Force and Scout interacted with. They had been born from a child's feelings of jealousy so were not subjected to the same rules.

Jacinta decided to stay quiet for the rest of the journey. She felt a bit uncomfortable, now that Calamity was aware of her surroundings.

Besides, Calamity had questions that needed answering, before they delivered her to her mum.

"What happened when I was in the cave?"

"We are not entirely sure. There was some stuff in a bucket that has been taken away for analysis. Judging by the state you were in when we found you, I believe you may have been exposed to some type of drug that has affected your ability to remember events," he replied.

"How did you find me, Jacinta?"

"I followed Lucas and he led me straight to you. Then I contacted Force and he saved you and the other kids."

"Thank you for being a good friend, Jacinta."

"You're welcome, Calamity."

Calamity threw her arm around Jacinta's waist and smiled happily. Jacinta was pleasantly surprised by Calamity's reaction, and placed her arm around Calamity's shoulder. They walked the rest of the way in silence.

Twenty-Seven

Loretta had been waiting on the veranda for a sign of her baby. She had not had any success with the GPS locator on the phone, and was unable to discover Force's location.

There was no way she could call him to find out where he was, as she had forgotten to write the number down, in her haste to give the phone to him. In her jumbled state, it never occurred to her to pull out his business card and phone his mobile instead. There had been word from Mrs. Landscombe that the other children had been found and rescued.

Before Loretta could head to the station, Mrs. Landscombe took great pleasure in telling her that Calamity had not been amongst them. Poor Loretta's stomach was knotted in fear, and she was sure she would throw up at any minute. It was getting very late, and she had never felt so helpless in her whole life.

For the first time in a very long time, Loretta prayed. She asked that her daughter be delivered safe and sound. She promised she would be a better mother, and spend more time with her daughter, if she was just given the opportunity. Loretta spent the afternoon making cups of tea she never drank, and wandering aimlessly around the house.

A couple of hours after Force had left, she decided she would get out of the dress the designer had given her to wear, and put her favourite shirt and pair of jeans on. She was just about to make herself another cup of tea, when a car she didn't recognise, came up her driveway. It pulled to a stop, and she watched as Jacinta's parents opened the doors and stepped out.

"Good afternoon, Miss Loretta, have you heard the news?" Jacinta's dad, Paul, shouted out to her.

"Yeah, I know they found the missing kids," Loretta called back.

"No, the news about Jacinta and Calamity," Jacinta's mum, Michelle, said.

"What news?" Loretta asked, running over to the railings.

"Jacinta found her. They are on their way home!" Paul yelled with excitement, as he and Michelle ran up the stairs two at a time.

"Is that true?" Loretta asked, afraid it was some kind of sick joke.

"Yes, she's coming home." Michelle assured her.

JEALOUSY MONSTERS

Loretta sobbed with relief. Michelle and Paul grabbed an arm each, and supported her body as her legs threatened to crumble beneath her.

"Let's get you to a chair," Michelle said kindly.

They helped her get settled, and Michelle asked permission to put the kettle on. She found her way to the kitchen and brewed a fresh pot of tea for the women and a mug of instant coffee for Paul. Michelle gave Loretta the details of the missing children being brought into the police station with Mr. Force.

"Some of the children in our daughters' class, were brought in with the children who had been kidnapped. They were so excited that they played a part in the rescue of the missing children. The kidnapped children were taken away for medical treatment, soon after their arrival at the police station, and the other children were taken aside for a medical check-up.

"Jacinta stayed behind to help find Calamity, who had not been with the other children when they had been found, although the kidnapped children *had* seen her with Ruby and Lucas. Paul and I just received word that the kids were returning home, and we wanted to be the ones to tell you, before the gossips could put their spin on events and give you exaggerated information."

"Thank you so much for your kindness," Loretta said, with tears in her eyes. She hadn't had someone think of her as a person, other than a reason to have a chinwag, in a long time. Actually, not since her husband had been alive. Loretta began regretting her decision to stay. She hadn't realised, until now, just how nasty the people in this town could be, and how little support she had received, since becoming a single mother.

If not for the kindness shown by Michelle and Paul, she might have decided to just pack up with her daughter and leave that day. Calamity was tough. She could make friends anywhere they lived. Loretta was a bit more sensitive, and hadn't noticed how lonely she had become, keeping to herself. The phone rang and Loretta excused herself as she picked up the cordless phone. Michelle felt the hairs on the nape of her neck stand up on their ends. That was always her cue that something special was about to happen.

"Hello, Loretta speaking."

"Hello, Mother, it's me, Calamity."

"Hey there, Baby. Are you okay? Where are you?"

"I'm fine, Mum. I'm on my way home."

Michelle glanced in the direction of the hills, and watched Force's head appear above the crest. She got to her feet, and said, "Loretta."

Loretta followed the direction of her eyes, and saw her daughter's silhouette in the distance. She dropped the phone then ran along the veranda and down the stairs outside Calamity's room. Loretta rushed to the fence line and called her daughter's name. Calamity hung up the phone, waved to her mum and ran towards her. They met in the paddock and hugged each other tightly. Calamity apologised for running away, while her mother apologised for chasing her away. They laughed at one another's attempt to make the other feel better.

Jacinta ran to her mum and dad too. Paul picked her up and spun her around, telling her how proud she had made them both. He then placed her on the ground so her mother could shower her with affection too. Michelle hugged her tightly, and kissed the top of her head.

Force loved bearing witness to moments like these. They were extremely rare, and he treasured these types of memories with all his heart. To be able to reunite a parent with their child, made all of the sacrifices he made on a daily basis, worth it. He planned on making his excuses to leave, once they had finished hugging one another, but Loretta had other ideas.

She looked over the top of Calamity's head, and insisted he stay with the five of them, so they could thank him, and celebrate the girls' safe return. He didn't know how to decline without offending her, so he agreed to hang around for a little while.

Loretta led them to the house, and settled them on the deck out the back. It was a lot larger than the front veranda, and had a stereo system hooked up for some background music. She kept the music low, so they could still hear each other when they talked.

Glasses were brought out for a celebratory drink: Cola for the kids, and a sparkling white wine for the adults. Loretta quickly cut up a salad, and defrosted some sausages in the microwave to cook on the barbecue.

"Loretta, would Calamity be allowed to stay over at our place on Friday night?" Michelle asked.

"Can I, please, Mum?" begged Calamity.

Loretta looked at her daughter's face with mixed emotions. She wanted to spend the night with Calamity herself, seeing as though it was her thirteenth birthday. She knew she had upset Calamity by agreeing to reschedule the photo shoot for the Saturday when she had promised to spend the day with her daughter.

Her most pressing thought, however, was the fact that Calamity could have remained missing forever. She would have had to spend the rest of her life, living without her beloved daughter. With that thought in mind, she said, "I think that is a great idea." What was one missed birthday out of many?

"There is one thing I think you should know before you make your final decision. We are getting a new foster boy tomorrow," inserted Paul.

"Is it Geoffrey?" Jacinta asked excitedly.

"Yes," said Paul with a smile.

She was thrilled that her parents were able to help one of the kids who had nowhere to go and she was getting a big brother. As they raised their glasses, they heard another car driving up the dirt road. It was April, Force's Gatherer friend.

Twenty-Eight

April pulled to a stop and exited the car. Their voices drifted to her, and she followed the sound towards the house. Loretta started to leave the group to receive her guest, when Force said, "Please stay with your daughter. I will go greet April, and bring her around for introductions. April is my brother's wife."

Force met April at the top of the stairs to the veranda out the front. Her blonde hair with caramel highlights was not pulled back into a ponytail like she normally wore it. Instead it fell across her face and down to just below her chest. She wore a blue linen dress and blue high-heeled sandals. Her sapphire coloured eyes twinkled with happiness and her plum coloured lips were curved in a welcoming grin.

"Hello, Liam. The children are settled in at *our special medical centre*, and are being treated before being reunited with their parents. I've also taken care of the memories of your kids," April said.

He marvelled at the speed with which she was able to work. Twelve kids in the matter of a couple of hours. Not bad. As she went to meet the two kids who had helped them catch the monsters and have them relocated, Force mentioned that she was supposedly married to his brother, Dr. Wade Force.

"How did this come about?" she enquired.

"Loretta kind of hit on me when I came home with her daughter, the first time. Calamity told her I was a doctor and I told her I was married."

"And the second time?" she asked, glimpsing his surface thoughts.

"She kind of took me by surprise and I found myself kissing her back."

"Oh, Force, when are you going to stop attracting the women?" she asked him with a sigh and placed her arm through his. They walked out the back together, and Force introduced April as his beautifully talented, federal agent sister- in-law.

The adults asked her questions regarding the welfare of the children who had been rescued. Then they requested information concerning the kidnappers, such as who they were and what was going to happen to them. April answered their questions as best she could. "Jacinta and Calamity, you have no idea how lucky you were," she concluded.

"Luck played no part in the events of the afternoon," Jacinta assured April in her confident manner.

April smiled at the spunk this one displayed, and quietly asked Force if he had alerted the guardians to this one's distinguishing traits. He assured her it was being taken care of, and that Guardian Karah would arrive very shortly to set things in place.

Scout wished she could pop out of Force's pocket, and say 'hello' to April. She really liked this Gatherer, and wondered if her Locator, Briella, was with her. She kept saying Force's name over and over in her mind to gain his attention.

'What is it, Scout?' he projected to her.

'Please say 'hi' to April for me, and can you ask her if Briella is here?'

'Yes, Briella is here. She is hiding under the house.'

'Can you walk over to the railings so I can fly down and spend some time with her?'

JEALOUSY MONSTERS

Force walked over to the railing with his drink, enabling Scout to make her escape unseen.

"Oh my goodness, look at you," Scout said, grabbing Briella by the arms and spinning her around. Her hair was lime green, and her eyes were like tiny emeralds. She wore a pair of long, lime green harem pants with an aqua waist band. Her lime green shirt was fastened together with a button in the middle of her breasts. Her ensemble was completed with off-white, slip-on shoes. "How did you change your colouring?"

"April. She has taken my love for colour to a whole new level. Sunday nights are spent with food colouring to change my hair colour, and she has become very clever at shrinking coloured contact lenses to fairy size."

"You look amazing," Scout said with wonder.

The fairies had loads of fun under the house, laughing and catching up on the missions they had both completed, since seeing each other last.

They spilled their guts on their Gatherers' failed attempts at staying under the radar, and the humans who had fallen for their good looks and charms.

"Are you and April currently working on a case?" Scout asked Briella.

"Yes. I'm tracking a vampire that is wickedly fast, and is not afraid to leave evidence of her feeding habits behind. She is obviously not trying to stay unnoticed, which is highly unusual, as you know."

"Can we help?" It had been quite a while since Scout had tracked a vampire and she thought it would be safer for April to have another Gatherer's eyes on the case. The last time Force had taken down a vampire, it had nearly been him that had been taken out. Scout had been so frightened, she decided she wouldn't tell him the next time she found one.

But knowing April, her next favourite Gatherer, would be out there on her own against a vampire, was enough to encourage Scout to tell her friend what had transpired the last time Force had come up against one, and offer his services. Briella listened to Scout's story, and agreed the two Gatherers should work together on this case.

April joined Force at the railing. "How lovely would it be to settle down in a place like this? The view is open and natural, unlike the city, and the aroma is so fresh and clean. I miss the country. I wonder if it would be possible to live here."

It didn't take long before she realised it wouldn't work very well. Most of the creatures they hunted lurked in the cities and coastlines where the human population was denser. Still, it might be worth considering purchasing a place somewhere like this for holidays.

Loretta informed them, "There is a place for sale ten kilometres west of here."

Paul said, "Michelle and I will be happy to contact the local real estate tomorrow. We'll see if we can't get you and your husband a discounted price, considering how Force has just cracked the kidnapping case. Why don't you and your husband stay the night? Oh, and of course, you too, Force," he added, thinking he may have been a bit rude.

April was disappointed to not be able to stay the night, with the possibility of viewing the property in the morning. She had a vampire to catch, and had to leave as soon as possible. The vampire would awaken soon, and would begin its hunt for human blood.

"Thank you so much for the invitation. We would love to stay but, unfortunately, Force and I need to go. We have some things to complete in relation to the case. However, I am really interested in buying a holiday place, and I would like to discuss the possibility of purchasing the property with my husband. I will be in touch in the morning to request a viewing if he agrees." April couldn't stop thinking about Force's desire to keep an eye on Jacinta, and become some sort of mentor for her. She wasn't sure if that would be a good thing or not.

JEALOUSY MONSTERS

April handed Loretta a card that contained the details of an appointment she had made for Calamity, at their medical centre the following day. She told her the centre had very good therapists, who would be able to assist Calamity with her traumatic experience.

Jacinta made them promise to come to see her again before they left for good. April and Force agreed to come back to say goodbye before they left town. They made their way to April's car. Scout and Briella flew to the car and, in the twilight, looked like two playful butterflies to the humans.

"Oh look, Force, two butterflies," she said as she opened the door, and they flew inside. "Should we try to get them out?"

"No, our skin might affect their wings and stop their ability to fly. Just put the windows down. They will fly out when they are ready."

They entered the car and waved goodbye. As they left, Paul and Michelle helped Loretta get the plates and cutlery ready for their impromptu barbeque. It had been a very long day.

April discussed her idea of purchasing the property together with Force, and he agreed it was a great idea. He thought it might be good for Scout as well. She would be safer living in a place like this, and there were forests on the outskirts of town, where she could recharge herself and feel closer to nature.

As long as he was able to relocate Scout's house to a secluded part of the property, he was happy to go halves with April. He also liked the idea of being able to keep an eye on Jacinta, from time to time.

April took Force to their medical centre, so he could see the work being done with the children. Geoffrey was going to be the hardest to help, as he was the first to be taken, and it was his emotions that had brought the creatures' to life in the first place.

They managed to spend fifteen minutes at the centre, before Guardian Karah announced her return. Force showed her the directions to Calamity's place, and confirmed he would meet her there. Force then asked April to give him a lift back, so he could beat Karah there, and pave the way for her visit.

The sun was sitting very low in the western sky, and April was concerned that she would not be able to reach the vampire, before it took its first victim of the night. Yet she agreed to drive him back. It wasn't dark enough for him to shift into another creature that would get him there before Karah.

Jacinta was excited to see that April and Force had come back like they said they would. She hoped they would soon become her neighbours. Jacinta imagined all sorts of fun things they could do together, when he was not capturing creatures. Of course they would have to be very careful, so Force's extra curricula activities were not discovered by the locals. Imagine the hullabaloo that would occur if they knew of his abilities. He would be locked up and studied by men and women in white coats. That was no life for someone as special as Force.

Before Jacinta could get too carried away and cause her parents to ask awkward questions about the reason for her excitability, Force told them the head of their division wanted a word with Jacinta, and would be arriving shortly.

"I'm so sorry that you weren't informed earlier, but I have just been told. Loretta, I hope you don't feel as though your home is being intruded upon. There is no necessity to do any preparation for her arrival."

Loretta waived his concerns aside, as did Michelle and Paul. They were happy to comply with whatever the government departments required, now that Calamity was safe. Guardian Karah knocked on the door making Jacinta jump in fright.

Twenty-Nine

"**F**eeling a bit skittish, Squirt?" her dad questioned. Jacinta smiled at him and nodded.

She didn't want to tell him about the pictures her mind had conjured, of creatures that could be walking the Earth, this very minute, feeding on and torturing the humans. She looked at Force to see if they were in danger, and was calmed by the carefree way he remained seated on the chair.

Loretta met Karah at the door, and invited her in. Karah made enquires as to Calamity's mood, and was told that she had fallen asleep on the hammock on the deck. Karah said a few calming words, before she asked Michelle and Paul if she could have a private word with Jacinta.

Her parents were happy to have Karah speak to their daughter, as long as Force was allowed to be present during the discussion. Guardian Karah agreed, and left her parents, Loretta and April to keep each other company, while Force and she took Jacinta to another room.

They got her settled before debriefing her on the day's events. Karah explained, "You will not be allowed to keep the memories of Force's abilities, and you will remember him only as a very competent investigator. Unfortunately, you won't be allowed to remember Scout at all."

Jacinta burst into tears. "Please don't take my memories. Instead of wiping them altogether, you could make me believe I had dreamed them instead." She implored Karah. At least that way she would think it wasn't real, but Force and Scout would still be remembered the way they really were.

"I am truly sorry, Jacinta. I have to erase the memories from your mind. It just isn't possible to allow you to keep them, for the safety of them both, if you should accidentally let something slip."

Jacinta cried. Karah gave her a few minutes to express the sadness that had enveloped her heart. Then she asked Jacinta to express her thoughts and feelings to Force, before her memories were removed.

"Thank you for everything Force. I wish I could have seen some of the other abilities you possess. What you do is amazing, and I want to thank you for making the world a safer place for us to grow up in. Please, remind Scout that it wasn't me who called her in front of my friends. It was Ruby pretending to be me. I would never have put her life in danger by letting others know of her existence. Tell her I love her, and I hope that she will be careful when seeking out the locations of the creatures you hunt.

"Please, help Calamity recover from this ordeal. She is not a bad person, and I wouldn't want her to suffer from issues for the rest of her days. Good bye, Force. I wish I was allowed to remember you," she said launching herself at him.

He grunted as she slammed into his torso, wrapping her arms around him in the fiercest hug he had ever received. A tear rolled down his cheek. She had really gotten to him and Karah looked on with concern. Was Force getting soft? Did she need to pull him out for a little while?

"You are a great kid, and there are still many adventures left in your childhood," Force told her. None of them, however, would compare to the adventures she would have as an adult. "Believe in yourself, and be kind to your friends." Then he handed her over to Karah.

Karah swiftly and adeptly removed the memories. She planted new memories to replace the gaps, so, if anyone asked her what had transpired, she would have a safe and believable account to give them. She then planted a hidden instruction for her to follow when she turned eighteen.

Karah told her to be at the old castle on the top of the hill in Westchester at midday, on All Hallows Eve. At that time she would meet Guardian Andromeda, who would open the portal that would enable her to begin her journey into the life as a Battle Star on Mystique.

Karah gently severed the connection between them, and viewed the young girl. Jacinta seemed calm and happy if not a little tired, which was to be expected. Karah asked Jacinta if she was ready to re-join the adults in the other room, and received an affirmative response. They left the bedroom, and made their way back to the lounge room.

Karah asked for a few words with her parents, and planted a series of scenarios in their heads. Jacinta would move away when she turned eighteen, and would be studying abroad. She created scenes that would be released at specific intervals throughout their lifetime, of holidays where the three of them got together to catch up with one another.

With each progressive scene, she aged their bodies to what she thought they might look like, to give it a touch of realism. Otherwise, the mind would fight against the memories, and would cause issues for the person owning them.

She wanted to give Jacinta's parents the illusion of a happy life. She had discovered they had already lost a daughter, and didn't want them to go through the pain of losing another. This was the better option, as far as she was concerned.

Once Karah had completed her task, she thanked them for their time. She spoke quietly to Loretta about Calamity's path to recovery, before excusing herself. Force and April walked Karah to the front of the building.

"Are you right to get home, Guardian?" Force asked.

"Yes, thank you, Force. I've got it all sorted," Karah assured him.

"Did everything go well with Jacinta and her parents?"

April asked, fishing for information.

"Yes, everything went well," Karah smiled, knowing what April was up to.

"Oh, crap. What about Geoffrey?" Force asked.

"I beg your pardon?" Karah quizzed.

"As soon as Geoffrey is released from hospital, he will be moving here as Paul and Michelle's foster child," Force explained. "Are the plans that you have set in motion for Jacinta going to have a negative effect on Geoffrey's life? He has had enough negatives to last him a lifetime, already."

Karah considered this new bit of information. Coming to a swift decision, she touched Force's face and said, "These are the memories I have implanted into Paul's and Michelle's minds. Perhaps sometime soon, you could modify them and implant the scenarios into Geoffrey's mind." The transfer of the implants from Karah's mind to Force's ensured there would be no misunderstandings or details left out, when Force completed the task.

"Thank you, Guardian Karah. I will take care of this in the next couple of days. May your journey be safe."

"Safe journey," April said.

Karah smiled at them both then walked down the stairs.

They watched her until she became lost to the darkness.

"Force, it's late," April reminded him.

"Sorry, April. Let's go say our goodbyes, and make tracks too."

Jacinta stood beside her parents, and waved goodbye to them. She didn't make a fuss as she didn't remember enough to feel the need to do so. Force felt pretty disappointed by the impersonal send off.

As they made their way to the car, April asked him if she could give him and Scout a lift anywhere.

"Nope, they are coming with us," Briella said fluttering in front of April's face.

JEALOUSY MONSTERS

"We are going to help them catch a vampire," Scout said, hovering in front of Force's face, with hands on hips and a huge grin on her face.

The Gatherers raced the Locators to the car. April put the car into gear, and put the pedal to the metal. Night had fallen, and the vampire was awake and hungry.

Titles by Marnie Atwell

Starlight Investigations

Jealousy Monsters

Vampire

Phantasm

Halloween Madness

The Pumpkin Patch

The House of Horrors

The Spirited Scarecrow

The Curious Kitten

About the Author

Marnie is an Australian author who lives in South-East Queensland with her husband and two children. When she is not dreaming up new adventures for her characters; Marnie enjoys writing, reading paranormal romance novels, and spending time with her family and friends. Not necessarily in that order.

Visit her website at: www.marnieatwell.com for more books, pictures, and downloads.

The next book in this series is:

Vampire